AF306743



Defoe
Abbott
Marx
Hardy
Melville
Montaigne
Machiavelli
Haggard
Chesterton
Cooper
Emerson
Joyce
Austen
Hugo
Eliot
Grimm
Stoker
Carroll
Christie
Maupassant
Byron
Molière
Wilde
Garnett
Einstein
Fitzgerald
Engels
Schiller
Smith
Kafka
Goethe
Hawthorne
Hall
Cotton
Dostoyevsky
Willis
Baum
Kipling
Doyle
Henry
Nietzsche
Leslie
Dumas
Flaubert
Turgenev
Balzac
Stockton
Vatsyayana
Crane
Burroughs
Verne
Curtis
Tocqueville
Vinci
Homer
Widger
Tolstoy
Gogol
Busch
Whitman
Darwin
Thoreau
Twain
Potter
Freud
Zola
Lawrence
Scott
Plato
Harte
Kant
Jowett
Stevenson
Dickens
Burton
Hesse
London
Andersen
Descartes
Cervantes
Poe
Aristotle
Wells
Voltaire
Cooke
Hale
James
Hastings
Bunner
Shakespeare
Irving
Richter
Chambers
da
Shaw
Doré
Chekhov
Benedict
Alcott
Dante
Pushkin
Swift
Wodehouse
Newton

# Lucretia

# Volume 2

Baron Edward Bulwer Lytton Lytton

# Imprint

This book is part of TREDITION CLASSICS

Author: Baron Edward Bulwer Lytton Lytton
Cover design: Buchgut, Berlin – Germany

Publisher: tredition GmbH, Hamburg - Germany
ISBN: 978-3-8424-3116-4

www.tredition.com
www.tredition.de

# CHAPTER III.

**CONFERENCES.**

The next day Sir Miles did not appear at breakfast,—not that he was unwell, but that he meditated holding certain audiences, and on such occasions the good old gentleman liked to prepare himself. He belonged to a school in which, amidst much that was hearty and convivial, there was much also that nowadays would seem stiff and formal, contrasting the other school immediately succeeding him, which Mr. Vernon represented, and of which the Charles Surface of Sheridan is a faithful and admirable type. The room that Sir Miles appropriated to himself was, properly speaking, the state apartment, called, in the old inventories, "King James's chamber;" it was on the first floor, communicating with the picture-gallery, which at the farther end opened upon a corridor admitting to the principal bedrooms. As Sir Miles cared nothing for holiday state, he had unscrupulously taken his cubiculum in this chamber, which was really the handsomest in the house, except the banquet-hall, placed his bed in one angle with a huge screen before it, filled up the space with his Italian antiquities and curiosities; and fixed his favourite pictures on the faded gilt leather panelled on the walls. His main motive in this was the communication with the adjoining gallery, which, when the weather was unfavourable, furnished ample room for his habitual walk. He knew how many strides by the help of his crutch made a mile, and this was convenient. Moreover, he liked to look, when alone, on those old portraits of his ancestors, which he had religiously conserved in their places, preferring to thrust his Florentine and Venetian masterpieces into bedrooms and parlours, rather than to dislodge from the gallery the stiff ruffs, doublets, and farthingales of his predecessors. It was whispered in the house that the baronet, whenever he had to reprove a tenant or lecture a dependant, took care to have him brought to his sanctum, through the full length of this gallery, so that the victim might be duly prepared and awed by the imposing effect of so stately a journey, and the grave faces of all the generations of St. John, which could not fail to impress him with the dignity of the family, and alarm him at the prospect of the injured frown of its representative. Across this gallery now, following the steps of the powdered valet, strode young Ardworth, staring now and then at some portrait more than usually grim, more often wondering why his boots, that never creaked before, should creak on those particular boards, and feeling a quiet curiosity, without the least mixture of fear or awe as to what old Squaretoes intended to say to him. But all feeling of irreverence ceased when, shown into the baronet's room, and the door closed, Sir Miles rose with a smile, and cordially shaking his hand, said, dropping the punctilious courtesy of Mister: "Ardworth, sir, if I had a little prejudice against you before you came, you have conquered it. You are a fine, manly, spirited fellow, sir; and you have an old man's good wishes, — which are no bad beginning to a young man's good fortune."

The colour rushed over Ardworth's forehead, and a tear sprang to his eyes. He felt a rising at his throat as he stammered out some not very audible reply.

"I wished to see you, young gentleman, that I might judge myself what you would like best, and what would best fit you. Your father is in the army: what say you to a pair of colours?"

"Oh, Sir Miles, that is my utmost ambition! Anything but law, except the
Church; anything but the Church, except the desk and a counter!"

The baronet, much pleased, gave him a gentle pat on the shoulder. "Ha, ha! we gentlemen, you see (for the Ardworths are very well born, very), we gentlemen understand each other! Between you and me, I never liked the law, never thought a man of birth should belong to it. Take money for lying, — shabby, shocking! Don't let that go any farther! The Church-Mother Church — I honour her! Church and State go together! But one ought to be very good to preach to others, — better than you and I are, eh? ha, ha! Well, then, you like the army, — there's a letter for you to the Horse Guards. Go up to town; your business is done. And, as for your outfit, — read this little book at your leisure." And Sir Miles thrust a pocketbook into Ardworth's hand.

"But pardon me," said the young man, much bewildered. "What claim have
I, Sir Miles, to such generosity? I know that my uncle offended you."

"Sir, that's the claim!" said Sir Miles, gravely. "I cannot live long," he added, with a touch of melancholy in his voice; "let me die in peace with all! Perhaps I injured your uncle, — who knows but, if so, he hears and pardons me now?"

"Oh, Sir Miles!" exclaimed the thoughtless, generous-hearted young man; "and my little playfellow, Susan, your own niece!"

Sir Miles drew back haughtily; but the burst that offended him rose so evidently from the heart, was so excusable from its motive and the youth's ignorance of the world, that his frown soon vanished as he said, calmly and gravely, —

"No man, my good sir, can allow to others the right to touch on his family affairs; I trust I shall be just to the poor young lady. And so, if we never meet again, let us think well of each other. Go, my boy; serve your king and your country!"

"I will do my best, Sir Miles, if only to merit your kindness."

"Stay a moment: you are intimate, I find, with young Mainwaring?"

"An old college friendship, Sir Miles."

"The army will not do for him, eh?"

"He is too clever for it, sir."

"Ah, he'd make a lawyer, I suppose, — glib tongue enough, and can talk well; and lie, if he's paid for it?"

"I don't know how lawyers regard those matters, Sir Miles; but if you don't make him a lawyer, I am sure you must leave him an honest man."

"Really and truly —"

"Upon my honour I think so."

"Good-day to you, and good luck. You must catch the coach at the lodge; for I see by the papers that, in spite of all the talk about peace, they are raising regiments like wildfire."

With very different feelings from those with which he had entered the room, Ardworth quitted it. He hurried into his own chamber to thrust his clothes into his portmanteau, and while thus employed, Mainwaring entered.

"Joy, my dear fellow, wish me joy! I am going to town, — into the army; abroad; to be shot at, thank Heaven! That dear old gentleman! Just throw me that coat, will you?"

A very few more words sufficed to explain what had passed to Mainwaring.
He sighed when his friend had finished: "I wish I were going with you!"


"Do you? Sir Miles has only got to write another letter to the Horse Guards. But no, you are meant to be something better than food for powder; and, besides, your Lucretia! Hang it, I am sorry I cannot stay to examine her as I had promised; but I have seen enough to know that she certainly loves you. Ah, when she changed flowers with you, you did not think I saw you, — sly, was not I? Pshaw! She was only playing with Vernon. But still, do you know, Will, now that Sir Miles has spoken to me so, that I could have sobbed, 'God bless you, my old boy!' 'pon my life, I could! Now, do you know that I feel enraged with you for abetting that girl to deceive him?"

"I am enraged with myself; and — "

Here a servant entered, and informed Mainwaring that he had been searching for him; Sir Miles requested to see him in his room. Mainwaring started like a culprit.

"Never fear," whispered Ardworth; "he has no suspicion of you, I'm sure. Shake hands. When shall we meet again? Is it not odd, I, who am a republican by theory, taking King George's pay to fight against the French? No use stopping now to moralize on such contradictions. John, Tom, — what's your name? — here, my man, here, throw that portmanteau on your shoulder and come to the lodge."

And so, full of health, hope, vivacity, and spirit, John Walter Ardworth departed on his career.

Meanwhile Mainwaring slowly took his way to Sir Miles. As he approached the gallery, he met Lucretia, who was coming from her own room. "Sir Miles has sent for me," he said meaningly. He had time for no more, for the valet was at the door of the gallery, waiting to usher him to his host. "Ha! you will say not a word that can betray us; guard your looks too!" whispered Lucretia, hurriedly; "afterwards, join me by the cedars." She passed on towards the staircase, and glanced at the large clock that was placed there. "Past eleven! Vernon is never up before twelve. I must see him before my uncle sends for me, as he will send if he suspects—" She paused, went back to her room, rang for her maid, dressed as for walking, and said carelessly, "If Sir Miles wants me, I am gone to the rectory, and shall probably return by the village, so that I shall be back about one." Towards the rectory, indeed, Lucretia bent her way; but half-way there, turned back, and passing through the plantation at the rear of the house, awaited Mainwaring on the bench beneath the cedars. He was not long before he joined her. His face was sad and thoughtful; and when he seated himself by her side, it was with a weariness of spirit that alarmed her.

"Well," said she, fearfully, and she placed her hand on his.

"Oh, Lucretia," he exclaimed, as he pressed that hand with an emotion that came from other passions than love, "we, or rather I, have done great wrong. I have been leading you to betray your uncle's trust, to convert your gratitude to him into hypocrisy. I have been unworthy of myself. I am poor, I am humbly born, but till I came here, I was rich and proud in honour. I am not so now. Lucretia, pardon me, pardon me! Let the dream be over; we must not sin thus; for it is sin, and the worst of sin,—treachery. We must part: forget me!"

"Forget you! Never, never, never!" cried Lucretia, with suppressed but most earnest vehemence, her breast heaving, her hands, as he dropped the one he held, clasped together, her eyes full of tears,—transformed at once into softness, meekness, even while racked by passion and despair.

"Oh, William, say anything,—reproach, chide, despise me, for mine is all the fault; say anything but that word 'part.' I have chosen you, I have sought you out, I have wooed you, if you will; be it so. I cling to you, you are my all,—all that saves me from—from myself," she added falteringly, and in a hollow voice. "Your love—you know not what it is to me! I scarcely knew it myself before. I feel what it is now, when you say 'part.'"

Agitated and tortured, Mainwaring writhed at these burning words, bent his face low, and covered it with his hands.

He felt her clasp struggling to withdraw them, yielded, and saw her kneeling at his feet. His manhood and his gratitude and his heart all moved by that sight in one so haughty, he opened his arms, and she fell on his breast. "You will never say 'part' again, William!" she gasped convulsively.

"But what are we to do?"

"Say, first, what has passed between you and my uncle."

"Little to relate; for I can repeat words, not tones and looks. Sir Miles spoke to me, at first kindly and encouragingly, about my prospects, said it was time that I should fix myself, added a few words, with menacing emphasis, against what he called 'idle dreams and desultory ambition,' and observing that I changed countenance,—for I felt that I did,—his manner became more cold and severe. Lucretia, if he has not detected our secret, he more than suspects my—my presumption. Finally, he said dryly, that I had better return home, consult with my father, and that if I preferred entering into the service of the Government to any mercantile profession, he thought he had sufficient interest to promote my views. But, clearly and distinctly, he left on my mind one impression,—that my visits here are over."

"Did he allude to me—to Mr. Vernon?"

"Ah, Lucretia! do you know him so little,—his delicacy, his pride?"

Lucretia was silent, and Mainwaring continued:—

"I felt that I was dismissed. I took my leave of your uncle; I came hither with the intention to say farewell forever."

"Hush! hush! that thought is over. And you return to your father's,—perhaps better so: it is but hope deferred; and in your absence I can the more easily allay all suspicion, if suspicion exist. But I must write to you; we must correspond. William, dear William, write often,—write kindly; tell me, in every letter, that you love me,—that you love only me; that you will be patient, and confide."

"Dear Lucretia," said Mainwaring, tenderly, and moved by the pathos of her earnest and imploring voice, "but you forget: the bag is always brought first to Sir Miles; he will recognize my hand. And to whom can you trust your own letters?"

"True," replied Lucretia, despondingly; and there was a pause. Suddenly she lifted her head, and cried: "But your father's house is not far from this,—not ten miles; we can find a spot at the remote end of the park, near the path through the great wood: there I can leave my letters; there I can find yours."

"But it must be seldom. If any of Sir Miles's servants see me, if—"

"Oh, William, William, this is not the language of love!"

"Forgive me,—I think of you!"

"Love thinks of nothing but itself; it is tyrannical, absorbing,—it forgets even the object loved; it feeds on danger; it strengthens by obstacles," said Lucretia, tossing her hair from her forehead, and with an expression of dark and wild power on her brow and in her eyes. "Fear not for me; I am sufficient guard upon myself. Even while I speak, I think,—yes, I have thought of the very spot. You remember that hollow oak at the bottom of the dell, in which Guy St. John, the Cavalier, is said to have hid himself from Fairfax's soldiers? Every Monday I will leave a letter in that hollow; every Tuesday you can search for it, and leave your own. This is but once a week; there is no risk here."

Mainwaring's conscience still smote him, but he had not the strength to resist the energy of Lucretia. The force of her character seized upon the weak part of his own,—its gentleness, its fear of inflicting pain, its reluctance to say "No,"—that simple cause of misery to the over- timid. A few sentences more, full of courage, confidence, and passion, on the part of the woman, of constraint and yet of soothed and grateful affection on that of the man, and the affianced parted.

Mainwaring had already given orders to have his trunks sent to him at his father's; and, a hardy pedestrian by habit, he now struck across the park, passed the dell and the hollow tree, commonly called "Guy's Oak," and across woodland and fields golden with ripening corn, took his way to the town, in the centre of which, square, solid, and imposing, stood the respectable residence of his bustling, active, electioneering father.

Lucretia's eye followed a form as fair as ever captivated maiden's glance, till it was out of sight; and then, as she emerged from the shade of the cedars into the more open space of the garden, her usual thoughtful composure was restored to her steadfast countenance. On the terrace, she caught sight of Vernon, who had just quitted his own room, where he always breakfasted alone, and who was now languidly stretched on a bench, and basking in the sun. Like all who have abused life, Vernon was not the same man in the early part of the day. The spirits that rose to temperate heat the third hour after noon, and expanded into glow when the lights shone over gay carousers, at morning were flat and exhausted. With hollow eyes and that weary fall of the muscles of the cheeks which betrays the votary of Bacchus,—the convivial three-bottle man,— Charley Vernon forced a smile, meant to be airy and impertinent, to his pale lips, as he rose with effort, and extended three fingers to his cousin.

"Where have you been hiding? Catching bloom from the roses? You have the prettiest shade of colour,—just enough; not a hue too much. And there is Sir Miles's valet gone to the rectory, and the fat footman puffing away towards the village, and I, like a faithful warden, from my post at the castle, all looking out for the truant."

"But who wants me, cousin?" said Lucretia, with the full blaze of her rare and captivating smile.

"The knight of Laughton confessedly wants thee, O damsel! The knight of the Bleeding Heart may want thee more,—dare he own it?"

And with a hand that trembled a little, not with love, at least, it trembled always a little before the Madeira at luncheon, — he lifted hers to his lips.

"Compliments again, — words, idle words!" said Lucretia, looking down bashfully.

"How can I convince thee of my sincerity, unless thou takest my life as its pledge, maid of Laughton?"

And very much tired of standing, Charley Vernon drew her gently to the bench and seated himself by her side. Lucretia's eyes were still downcast, and she remained silent; Vernon, suppressing a yawn, felt that he was bound to continue. There was nothing very formidable in Lucretia's manner.

"'Fore Gad!" thought he, "I suppose I must take the heiress after all; the sooner 't is over, the sooner I can get back to Brook Street."

"It is premature, my fair cousin," said he, aloud, — "premature, after less than a week's visit, and only some fourteen or fifteen hours' permitted friendship and intimacy, to say what is uppermost in my thoughts; but we spendthrifts are provokingly handsome! Sir Miles, your good uncle, is pleased to forgive all my follies and faults upon one condition, — that you will take on yourself the task to reform me. Will you, my fair cousin? Such as I am, you behold me. I am no sinner in the disguise of a saint. My fortune is spent, my health is not strong; but a young widow's is no mournful position. I am gay when I am well, good- tempered when ailing. I never betrayed a trust, — can you trust me with yourself?"

This was a long speech, and Charley Vernon felt pleased that it was over. There was much in it that would have touched a heart even closed to him, and a little genuine emotion had given light to his eyes, and color to his cheek. Amidst all the ravages of dissipation, there was something interesting in his countenance, and manly in his tone and his gesture. But Lucretia was only sensible to one part of his confession, — her uncle consented to his suit. This was all of which she desired to be assured, and against this she now sought to screen herself.

"Your candour, Mr. Vernon," she said, avoiding his eye, "deserves candour in me; I cannot affect to misunderstand you. But you take me by surprise; I was so unprepared for this. Give me time, — I must reflect."

"Reflection is dull work in the country; you can reflect more amusingly in town, my fair cousin."

"I will wait, then, till I find myself in town."

"Ah, you make me the happiest, the most grateful of men," cried Mr. Vernon, rising, with a semi-genuflection which seemed to imply, "Consider yourself knelt to," — just as a courteous assailer, with a motion of the hand, implies, "Consider yourself horsewhipped."

Lucretia, who, with all her intellect, had no capacity for humour, recoiled, and looked up in positive surprise.

"I do not understand you, Mr. Vernon," she said, with austere gravity.

"Allow me the bliss of flattering myself that you, at least, are understood," replied Charley Vernon, with imperturbable assurance. "You will wait to reflect till you are in town, — that is to say, the day after our honeymoon, when you awake in Mayfair."

Before Lucretia could reply, she saw the indefatigable valet formally approaching, with the anticipated message that Sir Miles requested to see her. She replied hurriedly to this last, that she would be with her uncle immediately; and when he had again disappeared within the porch, she said, with a constrained effort at frankness, —

"Mr. Vernon, if I have misunderstood your words, I think I do not mistake your character. You cannot wish to take advantage of my affection for my uncle, and the passive obedience I owe to him, to force me into a step of which — of which — I have not yet sufficiently considered the results. If you really desire that my feelings should be consulted, that I should not — pardon me — consider myself sacrificed to the family pride of my guardian and the interests of my suitor — "

"Madam!" exclaimed Vernon, reddening.

Pleased with the irritating effect her words had produced, Lucretia continued calmly, "If, in a word, I am to be a free agent in a choice on which my happiness depends, forbear to urge Sir Miles further at present; forbear to press your suit upon me. Give me the delay of a few months; I shall know how to appreciate your delicacy."

"Miss Clavering," answered Vernon, with a touch of the St. John haughtiness, "I am in despair that you should even think so grave an appeal to my honour necessary. I am well aware of your expectations and my poverty. And, believe me, I would rather rot in a prison than enrich myself by forcing your inclinations. You have but to say the word, and I will (as becomes me as a man and gentleman) screen you from all chance of Sir Miles's displeasure, by taking it on myself to decline an honour of which I feel, indeed, very undeserving."

"But I have offended you," said Lucretia, softly, while she turned aside to conceal the glad light of her eyes,—"pardon me; and to prove that you do so, give me your arm to my uncle's room."

Vernon, with rather more of Sir Miles's antiquated stiffness than his own rakish ease, offered his arm, with a profound reverence, to his cousin, and they took their way to the house. Not till they had passed up the stairs, and were even in the gallery, did further words pass between them. Then Vernon said,—

"But what is your wish, Miss Clavering? On what footing shall I remain here?"

"Will you suffer me to dictate?" replied Lucretia, stopping short with well-feigned confusion, as if suddenly aware that the right to dictate gives the right to hope.

"Ah, consider me at least your slave!" whispered Vernon, as, his eye resting on the contour of that matchless neck, partially and advantageously turned from him, he began, with his constitutional admiration of the sex, to feel interested in a pursuit that now seemed, after piquing, to flatter his self-love.

"Then I will use the privilege when we meet again," answered Lucretia; and drawing her arm gently from his, she passed on to her uncle, leaving Vernon midway in the gallery.

Those faded portraits looked down on her with that melancholy gloom which the effigies of our dead ancestors seem mysteriously to acquire. To noble and aspiring spirits, no homily to truth and honour and fair ambition is more eloquent than the mute and melancholy canvas from which our fathers, made, by death, our household gods, contemplate us still. They appear to confide to us the charge of their unblemished names. They speak to us from the grave, and heard aright, the pride of family is the guardian angel of its heirs. But Lucretia, with her hard and scholastic mind, despised as the veriest weakness all the poetry that belongs to the sense of a pure descent. It was because she was proud as the proudest in herself that she had nothing but contempt for the virtue, the valour, or the wisdom of those that had gone before. So, with a brain busy with guile and stratagem, she trod on, beneath the eyes of the simple and spotless Dead.

Vernon, thus left alone, mused a few moments on what had passed between himself and the heiress; and then, slowly retracing his steps, his eye roved along the stately series of his line. "Faith!" he muttered, "if my boyhood had been passed in this old gallery, his Royal Highness would have lost a good fellow and hard drinker, and his Majesty would have had perhaps a more distinguished soldier,—certainly a worthier subject. If I marry this lady, and we are blessed with a son, he shall walk through this gallery once a day before he is flogged into Latin!"

Lucretia's interview with her uncle was a masterpiece of art. What pity that such craft and subtlety were wasted in our little day, and on such petty objects; under the Medici, that spirit had gone far to the shaping of history. Sure, from her uncle's openness, that he would plunge at once into the subject for which she deemed she was summoned, she evinced no repugnance when, tenderly kissing her, he asked if Charles Vernon had a chance of winning favour in her eyes. She knew that she was safe in saying "No;" that her uncle would never force her inclinations,—safe so far as Vernon was concerned; but she desired more: she desired thoroughly to quench all suspicion that her heart was pre-occupied; entirely to remove from Sir Miles's thoughts the image of Mainwaring; and a denial of one suitor might quicken the baronet's eyes to the concealment of the other. Nor was this all; if Sir Miles was seriously bent upon seeing her settled in marriage before his death, the dismissal of Vernon might only expose her to the importunity of new candidates more difficult to deal with. Vernon himself she could use as the shield against the arrows of a host. Therefore, when Sir Miles repeated his question, she answered, with much gentleness and seeming modest sense, that Mr. Vernon had much that must prepossess in his favour; that in addition to his own advantages he had one, the highest in her eyes,—her uncle's sanction and approval. But—and she hesitated with becoming and natural diffidence—were not his habits unfixed and roving? So it was said; she knew not herself,—she would trust her happiness to her uncle. But if so, and if Mr. Vernon were really disposed to change, would it not be prudent to try him,—try him where there was temptation, not in the repose of Laughton, but amidst his own haunts of London? Sir Miles had friends who would honestly inform him of the result. She did but suggest this; she was too ready to leave all to her dear guardian's acuteness and experience.

Melted by her docility, and in high approval of the prudence which betokened a more rational judgment than he himself had evinced, the good old man clasped her to his breast and shed tears as he praised and thanked her. She had decided, as she always did, for the best; Heaven forbid that she should be wasted on an incorrigible man of pleasure! "And," said the frank-hearted gentleman, unable long to keep any thought concealed,—"and to think that I could have wronged you for a moment, my own noble child; that I could have been dolt enough to suppose that the good looks of that boy Mainwaring might have caused you to forget what— But you change colour!"—for, with all her dissimulation, Lucretia loved too ardently not to shrink at that name thus suddenly pronounced. "Oh," continued the baronet, drawing her still nearer towards him, while with one hand he put back her face, that he might read its expression the more closely,—"oh, if it had been so,—if it be so, I will pity, not blame you, for my neglect was the fault: pity you, for I have known a similar struggle; admire you in pity, for you have the spirit of your ancestors, and you will conquer the weakness. Speak! have I touched on the truth? Speak without fear, child,—you have no mother; but in age a man sometimes gets a mother's heart."

Startled and alarmed as the lark when the step nears its nest, Lucretia summoned all the dark wile of her nature to mislead the intruder. "No, uncle, no; I am not so unworthy. You misconceived my emotion."

"Ah, you know that he has had the presumption to love you, — the puppy! — and you feel the compassion you women always feel for such offenders? Is that it?"

Rapidly Lucretia considered if it would be wise to leave that impression on his mind. On one hand, it might account for a moment's agitation; and if Mainwaring were detected hovering near the domain, in the exchange of their correspondence, it might appear but the idle, if hopeless, romance of youth, which haunts the mere home of its object, — but no; on the other hand, it left his banishment absolute and confirmed. Her resolution was taken with a promptitude that made her pause not perceptible.

"No, my dear uncle," she said, so cheerfully that it removed all doubt from the mind of her listener; "but M. Dalibard has rallied me on the subject, and I was so angry with him that when you touched on it, I thought more of my quarrel with him than of poor timid Mr. Mainwaring himself. Come, now, own it, dear sir! M. Dalibard has instilled this strange fancy into your head?"

"No, 'S life; if he had taken such a liberty, I should have lost my librarian. No, I assure you, it was rather Vernon; you know true love is jealous."

"Vernon!" thought Lucretia; "he must go, and at once." Sliding from her uncle's arms to the stool at his feet, she then led the conversation more familiarly back into the channel it had lost; and when at last she escaped, it was with the understanding that, without promise or compromise, Mr. Vernon should return to London at once, and be put upon the ordeal through which she felt assured it was little likely he should pass with success.

# CHAPTER IV.

## GUY'S OAK.

Three weeks afterwards, the life at Laughton seemed restored to the cheerful and somewhat monotonous tranquillity of its course, before chafed and disturbed by the recent interruptions to the stream. Vernon had departed, satisfied with the justice of the trial imposed on him, and far too high-spirited to seek to extort from niece or uncle any engagement beyond that which, to a nice sense of honour, the trial itself imposed. His memory and his heart were still faithful to Mary; but his senses, his fancy, his vanity, were a little involved in his success with the heiress. Though so free from all mercenary meanness, Mr. Vernon was still enough man of the world to be sensible of the advantages of the alliance which had first been pressed on him by Sir Miles, and from which Lucretia herself appeared not to be averse. The season of London was over, but there was always a set, and that set the one in which Charley Vernon principally moved, who found town fuller than the country. Besides, he went occasionally to Brighton, which was then to England what Baiae was to Rome. The prince was holding gay court at the Pavilion, and that was the atmosphere which Vernon was habituated to breathe. He was no parasite of royalty; he had that strong personal affection to the prince which it is often the good fortune of royalty to attract. Nothing is less founded than the complaint which poets put into the lips of princes, that they have no friends,—it is, at least, their own perverse fault if that be the case; a little amiability, a little of frank kindness, goes so far when it emanates from the rays of a crown. But Vernon was stronger than Lucretia deemed him; once contemplating the prospect of a union which was to consign to his charge the happiness of another, and feeling all that he should owe in such a marriage to the confidence both of niece and uncle, he evinced steadier principles than he had ever made manifest when he had only his own fortune to mar, and his own happiness to trifle with. He joined his old companions, but he kept aloof from their more dissipated pursuits. Beyond what was then thought the venial error of too devout libations to Bacchus, Charley Vernon seemed reformed.

Ardworth had joined a regiment which had departed for the field of action. Mainwaring was still with his father, and had not yet announced to Sir Miles any wish or project for the future.

Olivier Dalibard, as before, passed his mornings alone in his chamber,— his noons and his evenings with Sir Miles. He avoided all private conferences with Lucretia. She did not provoke them. Young Gabriel amused himself in copying Sir Miles's pictures, sketching from Nature, scribbling in his room prose or verse, no matter which (he never showed his lucubrations), pinching the dogs when he could catch them alone, shooting the cats, if they appeared in the plantation, on pretence of love for the young pheasants, sauntering into the cottages, where he was a favourite because of his good looks, but where he always contrived to leave the trace of his visits in disorder and mischief, upsetting the tea-kettle and scalding the children, or, what he loved dearly, setting two gossips by the ears. But these occupations were over by the hour Lucretia left her apartment. From that time he never left her out of view; and when encouraged to join her at his usual privileged times, whether in the gardens at sunset or in her evening niche in the drawing- room, he was sleek, silken, and caressing as Cupid, after plaguing the Nymphs, at the feet of Psyche. These two strange persons had indeed apparently that sort of sentimental familiarity which is sometimes seen between a fair boy and a girl much older than himself; but the attraction that drew them together was an indefinable instinct of their similarity in many traits of their several characters,— the whelp leopard sported fearlessly around the she-panther. Before Olivier's midnight conference with his son, Gabriel had drawn close and closer to Lucretia, as an ally against his father; for that father he cherished feelings which, beneath the most docile obedience, concealed horror and hate, and something of the ferocity of revenge. And if young Varney loved any one on earth except himself, it was Lucretia Clavering. She had administered to his ruling passions, which were for effect and display; she had devised the dress which set off to the utmost his exterior, and gave it that picturesque and artistic appearance which he had sighed for in his study of the portraits of Titian and Vandyke. She supplied him (for in money she was generous) with enough to gratify and forestall every boyish caprice; and this liberality now turned against her, for it had increased into a settled vice his natural taste for extravagance, and made all other considerations subordinate to that of feeding his cupidity. She praised his drawings, which, though self-taught, were indeed extraordinary, predicted his fame as an artist, lifted him into consequence amongst the guests by her notice and eulogies, and what, perhaps, won him more than all, he felt that it was to her — to Dalibard's desire to conceal before her his more cruel propensities — that he owed his father's change from the most refined severity to the most paternal gentleness.

And thus he had repaid her, as she expected, by a devotion which she trusted to employ against her tutor himself, should the baffled aspirant become the scheming rival and the secret foe. But now, — thoroughly aware of the gravity of his father's objects, seeing before him the chance of a settled establishment at Laughton, a positive and influential connection with Lucretia; and on the other hand a return to the poverty he recalled with disgust, and the terrors of his father's solitary malice and revenge, — he entered fully into Dalibard's sombre plans, and without scruple or remorse, would have abetted any harm to his benefactress. Thus craft, doomed to have accomplices in craft, resembles the spider, whose web, spread indeed for the fly, attracts the fellow-spider that shall thrust it forth, and profit by the meshes it has woven for a victim, to surrender to a master.

Already young Varney, set quietly and ceaselessly to spy every movement of Lucretia's, had reported to his father two visits to the most retired part of the park; but he had not yet ventured near enough to discover the exact spot, and his very watch on Lucretia had prevented the detection of Mainwaring himself in his stealthy exchange of correspondence. Dalibard bade him continue his watch, without hinting at his ulterior intentions, for, indeed, in these he was not decided. Even should he discover any communication between Lucretia and Mainwaring, how reveal it to Sir Miles without forever precluding himself from the chance of profiting by the betrayal? Could Lucretia ever forgive the injury, and could she fail to detect the hand that inflicted it? His only hope was in the removal of Mainwaring from his path by other agencies than his own, and (by an appearance of generosity and self-abandonment, in keeping her secret and submitting to his fate) he trusted to regain the confidence she now withheld from him, and use it to his advantage when the time came to defend himself from Vernon. For he had learned from Sir Miles the passive understanding with respect to that candidate for her hand; and he felt assured that had Mainwaring never existed, could he cease to exist for her hopes, Lucretia, despite her dissimulation, would succumb to one she feared but respected, rather than one she evidently trifled with and despised.

"But the course to be taken must be adopted after the evidence is collected," thought the subtle schemer, and he tranquilly continued his chess with the baronet.

Before, however, Gabriel could make any further discoveries, an event occurred which excited very different emotions amongst those it more immediately interested.

Sir Miles had, during the last twelve months, been visited by two seizures, seemingly of an apoplectic character. Whether they were apoplexy, or the less alarming attacks that arise from some more gentle congestion, occasioned by free living and indolent habits, was matter of doubt with his physician,—not a very skilful, though a very formal, man. Country doctors were not then the same able, educated, and scientific class that they are now rapidly becoming. Sir Miles himself so stoutly and so eagerly repudiated the least hint of the more unfavourable interpretation that the doctor, if not convinced by his patient, was awed from expressing plainly a contrary opinion. There are certain persons who will dismiss their physician if he tells them the truth: Sir Miles was one of them.

In his character there was a weakness not uncommon to the proud. He did not fear death, but he shrank from the thought that others should calculate on his dying. He was fond of his power, though he exercised it gently: he knew that the power of wealth and station is enfeebled in proportion as its dependants can foresee the date of its transfer. He dreaded, too, the comments which are always made on those visited by his peculiar disease: "Poor Sir Miles! an apoplectic fit. His intellect must be very much shaken; he revoked at whist last night,—memory sadly impaired!" This may be a pitiable foible; but heroes and statesmen have had it most: pardon it

in the proud old man! He enjoined the physician to state throughout
the house and the neighbourhood that the attacks were wholly innocent and unimportant. The physician did so, and was generally
believed; for Sir Miles seemed as lively and as vigorous after them
as before. Two persons alone were not deceived,—Dalibard and
Lucretia. The first, at an earlier part of his life, had studied patholo-
gy with the profound research and ingenious application which he
brought to bear upon all he undertook. He whispered from the first
to Lucretia,—

"Unless your uncle changes his habits, takes exercise, and for-
bears wine and the table, his days are numbered."

And when this intelligence was first conveyed to her, before she
had become acquainted with Mainwaring, Lucretia felt the shock of
a grief sudden and sincere. We have seen how these better senti-
ments changed as human life became an obstacle in her way. In her
character, what phrenologists call "destructiveness," in the compre-
hensive sense of the word, was superlatively developed. She had
not actual cruelty; she was not bloodthirsty: those vices belong to a
different cast of character. She was rather deliberately and intellec-
tually unsparing. A goal was before her; she must march to it: all in
the way were but hostile impediments. At first, however, Sir Miles
was not in the way, except to fortune, and for that, as avarice was
not her leading vice, she could well wait; therefore, at this hint of
the Provencal's she ventured to urge her uncle to abstinence and
exercise. But Sir Miles was touchy on the subject; he feared the in-
terpretations which great change of habits might suggest. The
memory of the fearful warning died away, and he felt as well as
before; for, save an old rheumatic gout (which had long since left
him with no other apparent evil but a lameness in the joints that
rendered exercise unwelcome and painful), he possessed one of
those comfortable, and often treacherous, constitutions which
evince no displeasure at irregularities, and bear all liberties with
philosophical composure. Accordingly, he would have his own
way; and he contrived to coax or to force his doctor into an authority on his side: wine was necessary to his constitution; much exercise
was a dangerous fatigue. The second attack, following four months
after the first, was less alarming, and Sir Miles fancied it concealed
even from his niece; but three nights after his recovery, the old bar-

onet sat musing alone for some time in his own room before he retired to rest. Then he rose, opened his desk, and read his will attentively, locked it up with a slight sigh, and took down his Bible. The next morning he despatched the letters which summoned Ardworth and Vernon to his house; and as he quitted his room, his look lingered with melancholy fondness upon the portraits in the gallery. No one was by the old man to interpret these slight signs, in which lay a world of meaning.

A few weeks after Vernon had left the house, and in the midst of the restored tranquillity we have described, it so happened that Sir Miles's physician, after dining at the Hall, had been summoned to attend one of the children at the neighbouring rectory; and there he spent the night. A little before daybreak his slumbers were disturbed; he was recalled in all haste to Laughton Hall. For the third time, he found Sir Miles speechless. Dalibard was by his bedside. Lucretia had not been made aware of the seizure; for Sir Miles had previously told his valet (who of late slept in the same room) never to alarm Miss Clavering if he was taken ill. The doctor was about to apply his usual remedies; but when he drew forth his lancet, Dalibard placed his hand on the physician's arm.

"Not this time," he said slowly, and with emphasis; "it will be his death."

"Pooh, sir!" said the doctor, disdainfully.

"Do so, then; bleed him, and take the responsibility. I have studied medicine,—I know these symptoms. In this case the apoplexy may spare,— the lancet kills."

The physician drew back dismayed and doubtful.

"What would you do, then?"

"Wait three minutes longer the effect of the cataplasms I have applied.
If they fail—"

"Ay, then?"

"A chill bath and vigorous friction."

"Sir, I will never permit it."

24

"Then murder your patient your own way."

All this while Sir Miles lay senseless, his eyes wide open, his teeth locked. The doctor drew near, looked at the lancet, and said irresolutely, —

"Your practice is new to me; but if you have studied medicine, that's another matter. Will you guarantee the success of your plan?"

"Yes."

"Mind, I wash my hands of it; I take Mr. Jones to witness;" and he appealed to the valet.

"Call up the footman and lift your master," said Dalibard; and the doctor, glancing round, saw that a bath, filled some seven or eight inches deep with water, stood already prepared in the room. Perplexed and irresolute, he offered no obstacle to Dalibard's movements. The body, seemingly lifeless, was placed in the bath; and the servants, under Dalibard's directions, applied vigorous and incessant friction. Several minutes elapsed before any favourable symptom took place. At length Sir Miles heaved a deep sigh, and the eyes moved; a minute or two more, and the teeth chattered; the blood, set in motion, appeared on the surface of the skin; life ebbed back. The danger was passed, the dark foe driven from the citadel. Sir Miles spoke audibly, though incoherently, as he was taken back to his bed, warmly covered up, the lights removed, noise forbidden, and Dalibard and the doctor remained in silence by the bedside.

"Rich man," thought Dalibard, "thine hour is not yet come; thy wealth must not pass to the boy Mainwaring." Sir Miles's recovery, under the care of Dalibard, who now had his own way, was as rapid and complete as before. Lucretia when she heard, the next morning, of the attack, felt, we dare not say a guilty joy, but a terrible and feverish agitation. Sir Miles himself, informed by his valet of Dalibard's wrestle with the doctor, felt a profound gratitude and reverent wonder for the simple means to which he probably owed his restoration; and he listened, with a docility which Dalibard was not prepared to expect, to his learned secretary's urgent admonitions as to the life he must lead if he desired to live at all. Convinced, at last, that wine and good cheer had not blockaded out the enemy, and having to do, in Olivier Dalibard, with a very different temper from the doctor's, he assented with a tolerable grace to the trial of a strict regimen and to daily exercise in the open air. Dalibard now became constantly with him; the increase of his influence was as natural as it was apparent. Lucretia trembled; she divined a danger in his power, now separate from her own, and which threatened to be independent of it. She became abstracted and uneasy; jealousy of the Provencal possessed her. She began to meditate schemes for his downfall. At this time, Sir Miles received the following letter from Mr. Fielden: —

SOUTHAMPTON, Aug. 20, 1801.

DEAR SIR MILES, — You will remember that I informed you when I arrived at Southampton with my dear young charge; and Susan has twice written to her sister, implying the request which she lacked the courage, seeing that she is timid, expressly to urge, that Miss Clavering might again be permitted to visit her. Miss Clavering has answered as might be expected from the propinquity of the relationship; but she has perhaps the same fears of offending you that actuate her sister. But now, since the worthy clergyman who had undertaken my parochial duties has found the air insalubrious, and prays me not to enforce the engagement by which we had exchanged our several charges for the space of a calendar year, I am reluctantly compelled to return home, — my dear wife, thank Heaven, being already restored to health, which is an unspeakable mercy; and I am sure I cannot be sufficiently grateful to Providence, which has not only provided me with a liberal independence of more than 200 pounds a year, but the best of wives and the most dutiful of children, — possessions that I venture to call "the riches of the heart." Now, I pray you, my dear Sir Miles, to gratify these two deserving young persons, and to suffer Miss Lucretia incontinently to visit her sister. Counting on your consent, thus boldly demanded, I have already prepared an apartment for Miss Clavering; and Susan is busy in what, though I do not know much of such feminine matters, the whole house declares to be a most beautiful and fanciful toilet-cover, with roses and forget-me-nots cut out of muslin, and two large silk tassels, which cost her three shillings and fourpence. I cannot conclude without thanking you from my heart for your noble kindness to young Ardworth. He is so full of ardour and spirit that I remember, poor lad, when I left him, as I thought, hard at work on that well-known problem of Euclid vulgarly called the Asses' Bridge, — I found him describing a figure of 8 on the village pond, which was only just frozen over! Poor lad! Heaven will take care of him, I know, as it does of all who take no care of themselves. Ah, Sir Miles, if you could but see Susan, — such a nurse, too, in illness! I have the honour to be, Sir Miles, Your most humble, poor servant, to command, MATTHEW FIELDEN.

Sir Miles put this letter in his niece's hand, and said kindly, "Why not have gone to see your sister before? I should not have been angry. Go, my child, as soon as you like. To-morrow is Sunday, — no travelling that day; but the next, the carriage shall be at your order."

Lucretia hesitated a moment. To leave Dalibard in sole possession of the field, even for a few days, was a thought of alarm; but what evil could he do in that time? And her pulse beat quickly: Mainwaring could come to Southampton; she should see him again, after more than six weeks' absence! She had so much to relate and to hear; she fancied his last letter had been colder and shorter; she yearned to hear him say, with his own lips, that he loved her still. This idea banished or prevailed over all others. She thanked her uncle cheerfully and gayly, and the journey was settled.

"Be at watch early on Monday," said Olivier to his son.

Monday came; the baronet had ordered the carriage to be at the door at ten. A little before eight, Lucretia stole out, and took her way to Guy's Oak. Gabriel had placed himself in readiness; he had climbed a tree at the bottom of the park (near the place where hitherto he had lost sight of her); she passed under it, — on through a dark grove of pollard oaks. When she was at a sufficient distance, the boy dropped from his perch; with the stealth of an Indian he crept on her trace, following from tree to tree, always sheltered, always watchful. He saw her pause at the dell and look round; she descended into the hollow; he slunk through the fern; he gained the marge of the dell, and looked down, — she was lost to his sight. At length, to his surprise, he saw the gleam of her robe emerge from the hollow of a tree, — her head stooped as she came through the aperture; he had time to shrink back amongst the fern; she passed on hurriedly, the same way she had taken, back to the house; then into the dell crept the boy. Guy's Oak, vast and venerable, with gnarled green boughs below, and sere branches above, that told that its day of fall was decreed at last, rose high from the abyss of the hollow, high and far-seen amidst the trees that stood on the vantage-ground above,— even as a great name soars the loftier when it springs from the grave. A dark and irregular fissure gave entrance to the heart of the oak. The boy glided in and looked round; he saw nothing, yet something there must be. The rays of the early sun did not penetrate into the hollow, it was as dim as a cave. He felt slowly in every crevice, and a startled moth or two flew out. It was not for moths that the girl had come to Guy's Oak! He drew back, at last, in despair; as he did so, he heard a low sound close at hand,—a low, murmuring, angry sound, like a hiss; he looked round, and through the dark, two burning eyes fixed his own: he had startled a snake from its bed. He drew out in time, as the reptile sprang; but now his task, search, and object were forgotten. With the versatility of a child, his thoughts were all on the enemy he had provoked. That zest of prey which is inherent in man's breast, which makes him love the sport and the chase, and maddens boyhood and age with the passion for slaughter, leaped up within him; anything of danger and contest and excitement gave Gabriel Varney a strange fever of pleasure. He sprang up the sides of the dell, climbed the park pales on which it bordered, was in the wood where the young shoots rose green and strong from the underwood. To cut a staff for the strife, to descend again into the dell, creep again through the fissure, look round for those vengeful eyes, was quick done as the joyous play of the impulse. The poor snake had slid down in content and fancied security; its young, perhaps, were not far off; its wrath had been the instinct Nature gives to the mother. It hath done thee no harm yet, boy; leave it in peace! The young hunter had no ear to such whisper of prudence or mercy. Dim and blind in the fissure, he struck the ground and the tree with his stick, shouted out, bade the eyes gleam, and defied them. Whether or not the reptile had spent its ire in the first fruitless spring, and this unlooked-for return of the intruder rather daunted than exasperated, we leave those better versed in natural history to conjecture; but instead of obeying the challenge and courting the contest, it glided by the sides of the oak, close to the very feet of its foe, and emerging into the light, dragged its gray coils through the grass; but its hiss still betrayed it. Gabriel sprang through the fissure and struck at the craven, insulting it with a laugh of scorn as he struck. Suddenly it halted, suddenly reared its crest; the throat swelled with venom, the tongue darted out, and again, green as emeralds, glared the spite of its eyes. No fear felt Gabriel Varney; his arm was averted; he gazed, spelled and admiringly, with the eye of an artist. Had he had pencil and tablet at that moment, he would have dropped his weapon for the sketch, though the snake had been as deadly as the viper of Sumatra. The sight sank into his memory, to be reproduced often by the wild, morbid fancies of his hand. Scarce a moment, however, had he for the gaze; the reptile sprang, and fell, baffled and bruised by the involuntary blow of its enemy. As it writhed on the grass, how its colours came out; how graceful were the movements of its pain! And still the boy gazed, till the eye was sated and the cruelty returned. A blow, a second, a third,—all the beauty is gone; shapeless, and clotted with gore, that elegant head; mangled and dissevered the airy spires of that delicate shape, which had glanced in its circling involutions, free and winding as a poet's thought through his verse. The boy trampled the quivering relics into the sod, with a fierce animal joy of conquest, and turned once more towards the hollow, for a last almost hopeless survey. Lo, his object was found! In his search for the snake, either his staff or his foot had disturbed a layer of moss in the corner; the faint ray, ere he entered the hollow, gleamed upon something white. He emerged from the cavity with a letter in his hand; he read the address, thrust it into his bosom, and as stealthily, but more rapidly, than he had come, took his way to his father.

# CHAPTER V.

## HOUSEHOLD TREASON.

The Provencal took the letter from his son's hand, and looked at him with an approbation half-complacent, half-ironical. "Mon fils!" said he, patting the boy's head gently, "why should we not be friends? We want each other; we have the strong world to fight against."

"Not if you are master of this place."

"Well answered,—no; then we shall have the strong world on our side, and shall have only rogues and the poor to make war upon." Then, with a quiet gesture, he dismissed his son, and gazed slowly on the letter. His pulse, which was usually low, quickened, and his lips were tightly compressed; he shrank from the contents with a jealous pang; as a light quivers strugglingly in a noxious vault, love descended into that hideous breast, gleamed upon dreary horrors, and warred with the noxious atmosphere: but it shone still. To this dangerous man, every art that gives power to the household traitor was familiar: he had no fear that the violated seals should betray the fraud which gave the contents to the eye that, at length, steadily fell upon the following lines:—

DEAREST, AND EVER DEAREST,—Where art thou at this moment? What are thy thoughts,—are they upon me? I write this at the dead of night. I picture you to myself as my hand glides over the paper. I think I see you, as you look on these words, and envy them the gaze of those dark eyes. Press your lips to the paper. Do you feel the kiss that I leave there? Well, well! it will not be for long now that we shall be divided. Oh, what joy, when I think that I am about to see you! Two days more, at most three, and we shall meet, shall we not? I am going to see my sister. I subjoin my address. Come, come, come; I thirst to see you once more. And I did well to say, "Wait, and be patient;" we shall not wait long: before the year is out I shall be free. My uncle has had another and more deadly attack. I see its trace in his face, in his step, in his whole form and bearing. The only obstacle between us is fading away. Can I grieve when I think it, — grieve when life with you spreads smiling beyond the old man's grave? And why should age, that has survived all passion, stand with its chilling frown, and the miserable prejudices the world has not conquered, but strengthened into a creed, — why should age stand between youth and youth? I feel your mild eyes rebuke me as I write. But chide me not that on earth I see only you. And it will be mine to give you wealth and rank! Mine to see the homage of my own heart reflected from the crowd who bow, not to the statue, but the pedestal. Oh, how I shall enjoy your revenge upon the proud! For I have drawn no pastoral scenes in my picture of the future. No; I see you leading senates, and duping fools. I shall be by your side, your partner, step after step, as you mount the height, for I am ambitious, you know, William; and not less because I love, — rather ten thousand times more so. I would not have you born great and noble, for what then could we look to, — what use all my schemes, and my plans, and aspirings? Fortune, accident, would have taken from us the great zest of life, which is desire.

When I see you, I shall tell you that I have some fears of Olivier Dalibard; he has evidently some wily project in view. He, who never interfered before with the blundering physician, now thrusts him aside, affects to have saved the old man, attends him always. Dares he think to win an influence, to turn against me, — against us? Happily, when I shall come back, my uncle will probably be restored to the false strength which deceives him; he will have less need of Dalibard; and then — then let the Frenchman beware! I have already a plot to turn his schemes to his own banishment. Come to Southampton, then, as soon as you can, — perhaps the day you receive this; on Wednesday, at farthest. Your last letter implies blame of my policy with respect to Vernon. Again I say, it is necessary to amuse my uncle to the last. Before Vernon can advance a claim, there will be weeping at Laughton. I shall weep, too, perhaps; but there will be joy in those tears, as well as sorrow, — for then, when I clasp thy hand, I can murmur, "It is mine at last, and forever!"

Adieu! No, not adieu, — to our meeting, my lover, my beloved! Thy
                    LUCRETIA.

An hour after Miss Clavering had departed on her visit, Dalibard returned the letter to his son, the seal seemingly unbroken, and bade him replace it in the hollow of the tree, but sufficiently in sight to betray itself to the first that entered. He then communicated the plan he had formed for its detection,—a plan which would prevent Lucretia ever suspecting the agency of his son or himself; and this done, he joined Sir Miles in the gallery. Hitherto, in addition to his other apprehensions in revealing to the baronet Lucretia's clandestine intimacy with Mainwaring, Dalibard had shrunk from the thought that the disclosure would lose her the heritage which had first tempted his avarice or ambition; but now his jealous and his vindictive passions were aroused, and his whole plan of strategy was changed. He must crush Lucretia, or she would crush him, as her threats declared. To ruin her in Sir Miles's eyes, to expel her from his house, might not, after all, weaken his own position, even with regard to power over herself. If he remained firmly established at Laughton, he could affect intercession,—he could delay, at least, any precipitate union with Mainwaring, by practising on the ambition which he still saw at work beneath her love; he might become a necessary ally; and then—why, then, his ironical smile glanced across his lips. But beyond this, his quick eye saw fair prospects to self-interest: Lucretia banished; the heritage not hers; the will to be altered; Dalibard esteemed indispensable to the life of the baronet. Come, there was hope here,—not for the heritage, indeed, but at least for a munificent bequest.

At noon, some visitors, bringing strangers from London whom Sir Miles had invited to see the house (which was one of the lions of the neighbourhood, though not professedly a show-place), were expected. Aware of this, Dalibard prayed the baronet to rest quiet till his company arrived, and then he said carelessly,—

"It will be a healthful diversion to your spirits to accompany them a little in the park; you can go in your garden-chair; you will have new companions to talk with by the way; and it is always warm and sunny at the slope of the hill, towards the bottom of the park."

Sir Miles assented cheerfully; the guests came, strolled over the house, admired the pictures and the armour and the hall and the staircase, paid due respect to the substantial old-fashioned luncheon, and then, refreshed, and in great good-humour, acquiesced in Sir Miles's proposition to saunter through the park.

The poor baronet was more lively than usual. The younger people clustered gayly round his chair (which was wheeled by his valet), smiling at his jests and charmed with his courteous high-breeding. A little in the rear walked Gabriel, paying special attention to the prettiest and merriest girl of the company, who was a great favourite with Sir Miles, — perhaps for those reasons.

"What a delightful old gentleman!" said the young lady. "How I envy Miss
Clavering such an uncle!"


"Ah, but you are a little out of favour to-day, I can tell you," said Gabriel, laughingly; "you were close by Sir Miles when we went through the picture-gallery, and you never asked him the history of the old knight in the buff doublet and blue sash."

"Dear me, what of that?"

"Why, that was brave Colonel Guy St. John, the Cavalier, the pride and boast of Sir Miles; you know his weakness. He looked so displeased when you said, 'What a droll-looking figure!' I was on thorns for you!"

"What a pity! I would not offend dear Sir Miles for the world."

"Well, it's easy to make it up with him. Go and tell him that he must take you to see Guy's Oak, in the dell; that you have heard so much about it; and when you get him on his hobby, it is hard if you can't make your peace."

"Oh, I'll certainly do it, Master Varney;" and the young lady lost no time in obeying the hint. Gabriel had set other tongues on the same cry, so that there was a general exclamation when the girl named the subject,- -"Oh, Guy's Oak, by all means!"

Much pleased with the enthusiasm this memorial of his pet ancestor produced, Sir Miles led the way to the dell, and pausing as he reached the verge, said, —

"I fear I cannot do you the honours; it is too steep for my chair to descend safely."

Gabriel whispered the fair companion whose side he still kept to.

"Now, my dear Sir Miles," cried the girl, "I positively won't stir without you; I am sure we could get down the chair without a jolt. Look there, how nicely the ground slopes! Jane, Lucy, my dears, let us take charge of Sir Miles. Now, then."

The gallant old gentleman would have marched to the breach in such guidance; he kissed the fair hands that lay so temptingly on his chair, and then, rising with some difficulty, said, —

"No, my dears, you have made me so young again that I think I can walk down the steep with the best of you."

So, leaning partly on his valet, and by the help of the hands extended to him, step after step, Sir Miles, with well-disguised effort, reached the huge roots of the oak.

"The hollow then was much smaller," said he, "so he was not so easily detected as a man would be now, the damned crop-ears—I beg pardon, my dears; the rascally rebels—poked their swords through the fissure, and two went, one through his jerkin, one through his arm; but he took care not to swear at the liberty, and they went away, not suspecting him."

While thus speaking, the young people were already playfully struggling which should first enter the oak. Two got precedence, and went in and out, one after the other. Gabriel breathed hard. "The blind owlets!" thought he; "and I put the letter where a mole would have seen it!"

"You know the spell when you enter an oak-tree where the fairies have been," he whispered to the fair object of his notice. "You must turn round three times, look carefully on the ground, and you will see the face you love best. If I was but a little older, how I should pray—"

"Nonsense!" said the girl, blushing, as she now slid through the crowd, and went timidly in; presently she uttered a little exclamation.

The gallant Sir Miles stooped down to see what was the matter, and offering his hand as she came out, was startled to see her holding a letter.

"Only think what I have found!" said the girl. "What a strange place for a post-office! Bless me! It is directed to Mr. Mainwaring!"

"Mr. Mainwaring!" cried three or four voices; but the baronet's was mute. His eye recognized Lucretia's hand; his tongue clove to the roof of his mouth; the blood surged, like a sea, in his temples; his face became purple. Suddenly Gabriel, peeping over the girl's shoulder, snatched away the letter.

"It is my letter,—it is mine! What a shame in Mainwaring not to have come for it as he promised!"

Sir Miles looked round and breathed more freely.

"Yours, Master Varney!" said the young lady, astonished. "What can make your letters to Mr. Mainwaring such a secret?"

"Oh! you'll laugh at me; but—but—I wrote a poem on Guy's Oak, and Mr. Mainwaring promised to get it into the county paper for me; and as he was to pass close by the park pales, through the wood yonder, on his way to D— — last Saturday, we agreed that I should leave it here; but he has forgotten his promise, I see."

Sir Miles grasped the boy's arm with a convulsive pressure of gratitude. There was a general cry for Gabriel to read his poem on the spot; but the boy looked sheepish, and hung down his head, and seemed rather more disposed to cry than to recite. Sir Miles, with an effort at simulation that all his long practice of the world never could have nerved him to, unexcited by a motive less strong than the honour of his blood and house, came to the relief of the young wit that had just come to his own.

"Nay," he said, almost calmly, "I know our young poet is too shy to oblige you. I will take charge of your verses, Master Gabriel;" and with a grave air of command, he took the letter from the boy and placed it in his pocket.

The return to the house was less gay than the visit to the oak. The baronet himself made a feverish effort to appear blithe and debonair as before; but it was not successful. Fortunately, the carriages were all at the door as they reached the house, and luncheon being over, nothing delayed the parting compliments of the guests. As the last carriage drove away, Sir Miles beckoned to Gabriel, and bade him follow him into his room.

When there, he dismissed his valet and said, —

"You know, then, who wrote this letter. Have you been in the secret of the correspondence? Speak the truth, my dear boy; it shall cost you nothing."

"Oh, Sir Miles!" cried Gabriel, earnestly, "I know nothing whatever beyond this, — that I saw the hand of my dear, kind Miss Lucretia; that I felt, I hardly knew why, that both you and she would not have those people discover it, which they would if the letter had been circulated from one to the other, for some one would have known the hand as well as myself, and therefore I spoke, without thinking, the first thing that came into my head."

"You — you have obliged me and my niece, sir," said the baronet, tremulously; and then, with a forced and sickly smile, he added: "Some foolish vagary of Lucretia, I suppose; I must scold her for it. Say nothing about it, however, to any one."

"Oh, no, sir!"

"Good-by, my dear Gabriel!"

"And that boy saved the honour of my niece's name, — my mother's grandchild! O God! this is bitter, — in my old age too!"

He bowed his head over his hands, and tears forced themselves through his fingers. He was long before he had courage to read the letter, though he little foreboded all the shock that it would give him. It was the first letter, not destined to himself, of which he had ever broken the seal. Even that recollection made the honourable old man pause; but his duty was plain and evident, as head of the house and guardian to his niece. Thrice he wiped his spectacles; still they were dim, still the tears would come. He rose tremblingly, walked to the window, and saw the stately deer grouped in the distance, saw the church spire that rose above the burial vault of his ancestors, and his heart sank deeper and deeper as he muttered: "Vain pride! pride!" Then he crept to the door and locked it, and at last, seating himself firmly, as a wounded man to some terrible operation, he read the letter.

Heaven support thee, old man! thou hast to pass through the bitterest trial which honour and affection can undergo,—household treason. When the wife lifts high the blushless front and brazens out her guilt; when the child, with loud voice, throws off all control and makes boast of disobedience,—man revolts at the audacity; his spirit arms against his wrong: its face, at least, is bare; the blow, if sacrilegious, is direct. But when mild words and soft kisses conceal the worst foe Fate can arm; when amidst the confidence of the heart starts up the form of Perfidy; when out from the reptile swells the fiend in its terror; when the breast on which man leaned for comfort has taken counsel to deceive him; when he learns that, day after day, the life entwined with his own has been a lie and a stage-mime,—he feels not the softness of grief, nor the absorption of rage; it is mightier than grief, and more withering than rage,—it is a horror that appalls. The heart does not bleed, the tears do not flow, as in woes to which humanity is commonly subjected; it is as if something that violates the course of nature had taken place,—something monstrous and out of all thought and forewarning; for the domestic traitor is a being apart from the orbit of criminals: the felon has no fear of his innocent children; with a price on his head, he lays it in safety on the bosom of his wife. In his home, the ablest man, the most subtle and suspecting, can be as much a dupe as the simplest. Were it not so as the rule, and the exceptions most rare, this world were the riot of a hell!

And therefore it is that to the household perfidy, in all lands, in all ages, God's curse seems to cleave, and to God's curse man abandons it; he does not honour it by hate, still less will he lighten and share the guilt by descending to revenge. He turns aside with a sickness and loathing, and leaves Nature to purify from the earth the ghastly phenomenon she abhors.

Old man, that she wilfully deceived thee, that she abused thy belief and denied to thy question and profaned maidenhood to stealth,—all this might have galled thee; but to these wrongs old men are subjected,—they give mirth to our farces; maid and lover are privileged impostors. But to have counted the sands in thine hour-glass, to have sat by thy side, marvelling when the worms should have thee, and looked smiling on thy face for the signs of the death-writ—Die quick, old man; the executioner hungers for the fee!

There were no tears in those eyes when they came to the close; the letter fell noiselessly to the floor, and the head sank on the breast, and the hands drooped upon the poor crippled limbs, whose crawl in the sunshine hard youth had grudged. He felt humbled, stunned, crushed; the pride was clean gone from him; the cruel words struck home. Worse than a cipher, did he then but cumber the earth? At that moment old Ponto, the setter, shook himself, looked up, and laid his head in his master's lap; and Dash, jealous, rose also, and sprang, not actively, for Dash was old, too, upon his knees, and licked the numbed, drooping hands. Now, people praise the fidelity of dogs till the theme is worn out; but nobody knows what a dog is, unless he has been deceived by men,—then, that honest face; then, that sincere caress; then, that coaxing whine that never lied! Well, then,—what then? A dog is long-lived if he live to ten years,—small career this to truth and friendship! Now, when Sir Miles felt that he was not deserted, and his look met those four fond eyes, fixed with that strange wistfulness which in our hours of trouble the eyes of a dog sympathizingly assume, an odd thought for a sensible man passed into him, showing, more than pages of sombre elegy, how deep was the sudden misanthropy that blackened the world around. "When I am dead," ran that thought, "is there one human being whom I can trust to take charge of the old man's dogs?"

So, let the scene close!

# CHAPTER VI.

**THE WILL.**

The next day, or rather the next evening, Sir Miles St. John was seated before his unshared chicken,—seated alone, and vaguely surprised at himself, in a large, comfortable room in his old hotel, Hanover Square. Yes, he had escaped. Hast thou, O Reader, tasted the luxury of escape from a home where the charm is broken,—where Distrust looks askant from the Lares? In vain had Dalibard remonstrated, conjured up dangers, and asked at least to accompany him. Excepting his dogs and his old valet, who was too like a dog in his fond fidelity to rank amongst bipeds, Sir Miles did not wish to have about him a single face familiar at Laughton, Dalibard especially. Lucretia's letter had hinted at plans and designs in Dalibard. It might be unjust, it might be ungrateful; but he grew sick at the thought that he was the centre-stone of stratagems and plots. The smooth face of the Provencal took a wily expression in his eyes; nay, he thought his very footmen watched his steps as if to count how long before they followed his bier. So, breaking from all roughly, with a shake of his head and a laconic assertion of business in London, he got into his carriage,—his own old bachelor's lumbering travelling- carriage,—and bade the post-boys drive fast, fast! Then, when he felt alone,—quite alone,—and the gates of the lodge swung behind him, he rubbed his hands with a schoolboy's glee, and chuckled aloud, as if he enjoyed, not only the sense, but the fun of his safety; as if he had done something prodigiously cunning and clever.

So when he saw himself snug in his old, well-remembered hotel, in the same room as of yore, when returned, brisk and gay, from the breezes of Weymouth or the brouillards of Paris, he thought he shook hands again with his youth. Age and lameness, apoplexy and treason, all were forgotten for the moment. And when, as the excitement died, those grim spectres came back again to his thoughts, they found their victim braced and prepared, standing erect on that hearth for whose hospitality he paid his guinea a day,—his front proud and defying. He felt yet that he had fortune and power, that a movement of his hand could raise and strike down, that at the verge of the tomb he was armed, to punish or reward, with the balance and the sword. Tripped in the smug waiter, and announced "Mr. Parchmount."

"Set a chair, and show him in." The lawyer entered.

"My dear Sir Miles, this is indeed a surprise! What has brought you to town?"

"The common whim of the old, sir. I would alter my will."

Three days did lawyer and client devote to the task; for Sir Miles was minute, and Mr. Parchmount was precise, and little difficulties arose, and changes in the first outline were made, and Sir Miles, from the very depth of his disgust, desired not to act only from passion. In that last deed of his life, the old man was sublime. He sought to rise out of the mortal, fix his eyes on the Great Judge, weigh circumstances and excuses, and keep justice even and serene.

Meanwhile, unconscious of the train laid afar, Lucretia reposed on the mine, — reposed, indeed, is not the word; for she was agitated and restless that Mainwaring had not obeyed her summons. She wrote to him again from Southampton the third day of her arrival; but before his answer came she received this short epistle from London: —

"Mr. Parchmount presents his compliments to Miss Clavering, and, by desire of Sir Miles St. John, requests her not to return to Laughton. Miss Clavering will hear further in a few days, when Sir Miles has concluded the business that has brought him to London."

This letter, if it excited much curiosity, did not produce alarm. It was natural that Sir Miles should be busy in winding up his affairs; his journey to London for that purpose was no ill omen to her prospects, and her thoughts flew back to the one subject that tyrannized over them. Mainwaring's reply, which came two days afterwards, disquieted her much more. He had not found the letter she had left for him in the tree. He was full of apprehensions; he condemned the imprudence of calling on her at Mr. Fielden's; he begged her to renounce the idea of such a risk. He would return again to Guy's Oak and search more narrowly: had she changed the spot where the former letters were placed? Yet now, not even the non-receipt of her letter, which she ascribed to the care with which she had concealed it amidst the dry leaves and moss, disturbed her so much as the evident constraint with which Mainwaring wrote, — the cautious and lukewarm remonstrance which answered her passionate appeal. It may be that her very doubts, at times, of Mainwaring's affection had increased the ardour of her own attachment; for in some natures the excitement of fear deepens love more than the calmness of trust. Now with the doubt for the first time flashed the resentment, and her answer to Mainwaring was vehement and imperious. But the next day came a messenger express from London, with a letter from Mr. Parchmount that arrested for the moment even the fierce current of love.

When the task had been completed, — the will signed, sealed, and delivered, — the old man had felt a load lifted from his heart. Three or four of his old friends, bons vivants like himself, had seen his arrival duly proclaimed in the newspapers, and had hastened to welcome him. Warmed by the genial sight of faces associated with the frank joys of his youth, Sir Miles, if he did not forget the prudent counsels of Dalibard, conceived a proud bitterness of joy in despising them. Why take such care of the worn-out carcass? His will was made. What was left to life so peculiarly attractive? He invited his friends to a feast worthy of old. Seasoned revellers were they, with a free gout for a vent to all indulgence. So they came; and they drank, and they laughed, and they talked back their young days. They saw not the nervous irritation, the strain on the spirits, the heated membrane of the brain, which made Sir Miles the most jovial of all. It was a night of nights; the old fellows were lifted back into their chariots or sedans. Sir Miles alone seemed as steady and sober as if he had supped with Diogenes. His servant, whose respectful admonitions had been awed into silence, lent him his arm to bed, but Sir Miles scarcely touched it. The next morning, when the servant (who slept in the same room) awoke, to his surprise the glare of a candle streamed on his eyes. He rubbed them: could he see right? Sir Miles was seated at the table; he must have got up and lighted a candle to write, — noiselessly, indeed. The servant looked and looked, and the stillness of Sir Miles awed him: he was seated on an armchair, leaning back. As awe succeeded to suspicion, he sprang up, approached his master, took his hand: it was cold, and fell heavily from his clasp. Sir Miles must have been dead for hours.

The pen lay on the ground, where it had dropped from the hand; the letter on the table was scarcely commenced: the words ran thus, —

"LUCRETIA, — You will return no more to my house. You are free as if I were dead; but I shall be just. Would that I had been so to your mother, to your sister! But I am old now, as you say, and — "

To one who could have seen into that poor proud heart at the moment the hand paused forever, what remained unwritten would have been clear. There was, first, the sharp struggle to conquer loathing repugnance, and address at all the false and degraded one; then came the sharp sting of ingratitude; then the idea of the life grudged and the grave desired; then the stout victory over scorn, the resolution to be just; then the reproach of the conscience that for so far less an offence the sister had been thrown aside, the comfort, perhaps, found in her gentle and neglected child obstinately repelled; then the conviction of all earthly vanity and nothingness, — the look on into life, with the chilling sentiment that affection was gone, that he could never trust again, that he was too old to open his arms to new ties; and then, before felt singly, all these thoughts united, and snapped the cord.

In announcing his mournful intelligence, with more feeling than might have been expected from a lawyer (but even his lawyer loved Sir Miles), Mr. Parchmount observed that "as the deceased lay at a hotel, and as Miss Clavering's presence would not be needed in the performance of the last rites, she would probably forbear the journey to town. Nevertheless, as it was Sir Miles's wish that the will should be opened as soon as possible after his death, and it would doubtless contain instructions as to his funeral, it would be well that Miss Clavering and her sister should immediately depute some one to attend the reading of the testament on their behalf. Perhaps Mr. Fielden would kindly undertake that melancholy office."

To do justice to Lucretia, it must be said that her first emotions, on the receipt of this letter, were those of a poignant and remorseful grief, for which she was unprepared. But how different it is to count on what shall follow death, and to know that death has come! Susan's sobbing sympathy availed not, nor Mr. Fielden's pious and tearful exhortations; her own sinful thoughts and hopes came back to her, haunting and stern as furies. She insisted at first upon going to London, gazing once more on the clay,—nay, the carriage was at the door, for all yielded to her vehemence; but then her heart misgave her: she did not dare to face the dead. Conscience waved her back from the solemn offices of nature; she hid her face with her hands, shrank again into her room; and Mr. Fielden, assuming unbidden the responsibility, went alone.

Only Vernon (summoned from Brighton), the good clergyman, and the lawyer, to whom, as sole executor, the will was addressed, and in whose custody it had been left, were present when the seal of the testament was broken. The will was long, as is common when the dust that it disposes of covers some fourteen or fifteen thousand acres. But out of the mass of technicalities and repetitions these points of interest rose salient: To Charles Vernon, of Vernon Grange, Esq., and his heirs by him lawfully begotten, were left all the lands and woods and manors that covered that space in the Hampshire map known by the name of the "Laughton property," on condition that he and his heirs assumed the name and arms of St. John; and on the failure of Mr. Vernon's issue, the estate passed, first (with the same conditions) to the issue of Susan Mivers; next to that of Lucretia Clavering. There the entail ceased; and the contingency fell to the rival ingenuity of lawyers in hunting out, amongst the remote and forgotten descendants of some ancient St. John, the heir-at-law. To Lucretia Clavering, without a word of endearment, was bequeathed 10,000 pounds,—the usual portion which the house of St. John had allotted to its daughters; to Susan Mivers the same sum, but with the addition of these words, withheld from her sister: "and my blessing!" To Olivier Dalibard an annuity of 200 pounds a year; to Honore Gabriel Varney, 3,000 pounds; to the Rev. Matthew Fielden, 4,000 pounds; and the same sum to John Walter Ardworth. To his favourite servant, Henry Jones, an ample provision, and the charge of his dogs Dash and Ponto, with an allowance therefor, to be paid weekly, and cease at their deaths. Poor old man! he made it the interest of their guardian not to grudge their lease of life. To his other attendants, suitable and munificent bequests, proportioned to the length of their services. For his body, he desired it to be buried in the vault of his ancestors without pomp, but without a pretence to a humility which he had not manifested in life; and he requested that a small miniature in his writing-desk should be placed in his coffin. That last injunction was more than a sentiment,—it bespoke the moral conviction of the happiness the original might have conferred on his life. Of that happiness his pride had deprived him; nor did he repent, for he had deemed pride a duty. But the mute likeness, buried in his grave,—that told the might of the sacrifice he had made! Death removes all distinctions, and in the coffin the Lord of Laughton might choose his partner.

When the will had been read, Mr. Parchmount produced two letters, one addressed, in the hand of the deceased, to Mr. Vernon, the other in the lawyer's own hand to Miss Clavering. The last enclosed the fragment found on Sir Miles's table, and her own letter to Mainwaring, redirected to her in Sir Miles's boldest and stateliest autograph. He had, no doubt, meant to return it in the letter left uncompleted.

The letter to Vernon contained a copy of Lucretia's fatal epistle, and the following lines to Vernon himself:—

MY DEAR CHARLES,—With much deliberation, and with natural reluctance to reveal to you my niece's shame, I feel it my duty to transmit to you the accompanying enclosure, copied from the original with my own hand, which the task sullied.

I do so first, because otherwise you might, as I should have done in your place, feel bound in honour to persist in the offer of your hand,—feel bound the more, because Miss Clavering is not my heiress; secondly, because had her attachment been stronger than her interest, and she had refused your offer, you might still have deemed her hardly and capriciously dealt with by me, and not only sought to augment her portion, but have profaned the house of my ancestors by receiving her there as an honoured and welcome relative and guest. Now, Charles Vernon, I believe, to the utmost of my poor judgment, I have done what is right and just. I have taken into consideration that this young person has been brought up as a daughter of my house, and what the daughters of my house have received, I bequeath her. I put aside, as far as I can, all resentment of mere family pride; I show that I do so, when I repair my harshness to my poor sister, and leave both her children the same provision. And if you exceed what I have done for Lucretia, unless, on more dispassionate consideration than I can give, you conscientiously think me wrong, you insult my memory—and impugn my justice. Be it in this as your conscience dictates; but I entreat, I adjure, I command, at least that you never knowingly admit by a hearth, hitherto sacred to unblemished truth and honour, a person who has desecrated it with treason. As gentleman to gentleman, I impose on you this solemn injunction. I could have wished to leave that young woman's children barred from the entail; but our old tree has so few branches! You are unwedded; Susan too. I must take my chance that Miss Clavering's children, if ever they inherit, do not imitate the mother. I conclude she will wed that Mainwaring; her children will have a low-born father. Well, her race at least is pure,—Clavering and St. John are names to guarantee faith and honour; yet you see what she is! Charles Vernon, if her issue inherit the soul of gentlemen, it must come, after all, not from the well-born mother! I have lived to say this,—I who— But perhaps if we had looked more closely into the pedigree of those Claverings—.

Marry yourself,—marry soon, Charles Vernon, my dear kinsman; keep the old house in the old line, and true to its old fame. Be kind and good to my poor; don't strain on the tenants. By the way, Farmer Strongbow owes three years' rent,—I forgive him. Pension him off; he can do no good to the land, but he was born on it, and must not fall on the parish. But to be kind and good to the poor, not to strain the tenants, you must learn not to waste, my dear Charles. A needy man can never be generous without being unjust. How give, if you are in debt? You will think of this now,- -now,—while your good heart is soft, while your feelings are moved. Charley Vernon, I think you will shed a tear when you see my armchair still and empty. And I would have left you the care of my dogs, but you are thoughtless, and will go much to London, and they are used to the country now. Old Jones will have a cottage in the village,—he has promised to live there; drop in now and then, and see poor Ponto and Dash. It is late, and old friends come to dine here. So, if anything happens to me, and we don't meet again, good-by, and God bless you.

Your affectionate kinsman, MILES ST. JOHN.

# CHAPTER VII.

**THE ENGAGEMENT.**

It is somewhat less than three months after the death of Sir Miles St. John; November reigns in London. And "reigns" seems scarcely a metaphorical expression as applied to the sullen, absolute sway which that dreary month (first in the dynasty of Winter) spreads over the passive, dejected city.

Elsewhere in England, November is no such gloomy, grim fellow as he is described. Over the brown glebes and changed woods in the country, his still face looks contemplative and mild; and he has soft smiles, too, at times,—lighting up his taxed vassals the groves; gleaming where the leaves still cling to the boughs, and reflected in dimples from the waves which still glide free from his chains. But as a conqueror who makes his home in the capital, weighs down with hard policy the mutinous citizens long ere his iron influence is felt in the province, so the first tyrant of Winter has only rigour and frowns for London. The very aspect of the wayfarers has the look of men newly enslaved: cloaked and muffled, they steal to and fro through the dismal fogs. Even the children creep timidly through the streets; the carriages go cautious and hearse-like along; daylight is dim and obscure; the town is not filled, nor the brisk mirth of Christmas commenced; the unsocial shadows flit amidst the mist, like men on the eve of a fatal conspiracy. Each other month in London has its charms for the experienced. Even from August to October, when The Season lies dormant, and Fashion forbids her sons to be seen within hearing of Bow, the true lover of London finds pleasure still at hand, if he search for her duly. There are the early walks through the parks and green Kensington Gardens, which now change their character of resort, and seem rural and country-like, but yet with more life than the country; for on the benches beneath the trees, and along the sward, and up the malls, are living beings enough to interest the eye and divert the thoughts, if you are a guesser into character, and amateur of the human face,—fresh nursery-maid and playful children; and the old shabby-genteel, buttoned- up officer, musing on half-pay, as he sits alone in some alcove of Kenna, or leans pensive over the rail of the vacant Ring; and early tradesman, or clerk from the suburban lodging, trudging brisk to his business,—for business never ceases in London. Then at noon, what delight to escape to the banks at Putney or Richmond,—the row up the river; the fishing punt; the ease at your inn till dark! or if this tempt not, still Autumn shines clear and calm over the roofs, where the smoke has a holiday; and how clean gleam the vistas through the tranquillized thoroughfares; and as you saunter along, you have all London to yourself, Andrew Selkirk, but with the mart of the world for your desert. And when October comes on, it has one characteristic of spring,—life busily returns to the city; you see the shops bustling up, trade flowing back. As birds scent the April, so the children of commerce plume their wings and prepare for the first slack returns of the season. But November! Strange the taste, stout the lungs, grief-defying the heart, of the visitor who finds charms and joy in a London November.

In a small lodging-house in Bulstrode Street, Manchester Square, grouped a family in mourning who had had the temerity to come to town in November, for the purpose, no doubt, of raising their spirits. In the dull, small drawing-room of the dull, small house we introduce to you, first, a middle-aged gentleman whose dress showed what dress now fails to show,—his profession. Nobody could mistake the cut of the cloth and the shape of the hat, for he had just come in from a walk, and not from discourtesy, but abstraction, the broad brim still shadowed his pleasant, placid face. Parson spoke out in him, from beaver to buckle. By the coal fire, where, through volumes of smoke, fussed and flickered a pretension to flame, sat a middle-aged lady, whom, without being a conjurer, you would pronounce at once to be wife to the parson; and sundry children sat on stools all about her, with one book between them, and a low whispered murmur from their two or three pursed-up lips, announcing that that book was superfluous. By the last of three dim- looking windows, made dimmer by brown moreen draperies, edged genteelly with black cotton velvet, stood a girl of very soft and pensive expression of features,—pretty unquestionably, excessively pretty; but there was something so delicate and elegant about her,—the bend of her head, the shape of her slight figure, the little fair hands crossed one on each other, as the face mournfully and listlessly turned to the window, that "pretty" would have seemed a word of praise too often proffered to milliner and serving-maid. Nevertheless, it was perhaps the right one: "handsome" would have implied something statelier and more commanding; "beautiful," greater regularity of feature, or richness of colouring. The parson, who since his entrance had been walking up and down the small room with his hands behind him, glanced now and then at the young lady, but not speaking, at length paused from that monotonous exercise by the chair of his wife, and touched her shoulder. She stopped from her work, which, more engrossing than elegant, was nothing less than what is technically called "the taking in" of a certain blue jacket, which was about to pass from Matthew, the eldest born, to David, the second, and looked up at her husband affectionately. Her husband, however, spoke not; he only made a sign, partly with his eyebrow, partly with a jerk of his thumb over his right shoulder, in the direction of the young lady we have described, and then completed the pantomime with a melancholy shake of the head. The wife turned round and looked hard, the scissors horizontally raised in one hand, while the other reposed on the cuff of the jacket. At this moment a low knock was heard at the street- door. The worthy pair saw the girl shrink back, with a kind of tremulous movement; presently there came the sound of a footstep below, the creak of a hinge on the ground-floor, and again all was silent.

"That is Mr. Mainwaring's knock," said one of the children.

The girl left the room abruptly, and, light as was her step, they heard her steal up the stairs.

"My dears," said the parson, "it wants an hour yet to dark; you may go and walk in the square."

"'T is so dull in that ugly square, and they won't let us into the green. I am sure we'd rather stay here," said one of the children, as spokesman for the rest; and they all nestled closer round the hearth.

"But, my dears," said the parson, simply, "I want to talk alone with your mother. However, if you like best to go and keep quiet in your own room, you may do so."

"Or we can go into Susan's?"

"No," said the parson; "you must not disturb Susan."

"She never used to care about being disturbed. I wonder what's come to her?"

The parson made no rejoinder to this half-petulant question. The children consulted together a moment, and resolved that the square, though so dull, was less dull than their own little attic. That being decided, it was the mother's turn to address them. And though Mr. Fielden was as anxious and fond as most fathers, he grew a little impatient before comforters, kerchiefs, and muffettees were arranged, and minute exordiums as to the danger of crossing the street, and the risk of patting strange dogs, etc., were half-way concluded; with a shrug and a smile, he at length fairly pushed out the children, shut the door, and drew his chair close to his wife's.

"My dear," he began at once, "I am extremely uneasy about that poor girl."

"What, Miss Clavering? Indeed, she eats almost nothing at all, and sits so moping alone; but she sees Mr. Mainwaring every day. What can we do? She is so proud, I'm afraid of her."

"My dear, I was not thinking of Miss Clavering, though I did not interrupt you, for it is very true that she is much to be pitied."

"And I am sure it was for her sake alone that you agreed to Susan's request, and got Blackman to do duty for you at the vicarage, while we all came up here, in hopes London town would divert her. We left all at sixes and sevens; and I should not at all wonder if John made away with the apples."

"But, I say," resumed the parson, without heeding that mournful foreboding, — "I say, I was then only thinking of Susan. You see how pale and sad she is grown."

"Why, she is so very soft-hearted, and she must feel for her sister."

"But her sister, though she thinks much, and keeps aloof from us, is not sad herself, only reserved. On the contrary. I believe she has now got over even poor Sir Miles's death." "And the loss of the great property!"

"Fie, Mary!" said Mr. Fielden, almost austerely.

Mary looked down, rebuked, for she was not one of the high-spirited wives who despise their husbands for goodness.

"I beg pardon, my dear," she said meekly; "it was very wrong in me; but I cannot—do what I will—I cannot like that Miss Clavering."

"The more need to judge her with charity. And if what I fear is the case, I'm sure we can't feel too much compassion for the poor blinded young lady."

"Bless my heart, Mr. Fielden, what is it you mean?"

The parson looked round, to be sure the door was quite closed, and replied, in a whisper: "I mean, that I fear William Mainwaring loves, not Lucretia, but Susan."

The scissors fell from the hand of Mrs. Fielden; and though one point stuck in the ground, and the other point threatened war upon flounces and toes, strange to say, she did not even stoop to remove the chevaux-de- frise.

"Why, then, he's a most false-hearted young man!"

"To blame, certainly," said Fielden; "I don't say to the contrary,—though I like the young man, and am sure that he's more timid than false. I may now tell you—for I want your advice, Mary—what I kept secret before. When Mainwaring visited us, many months ago, at Southampton, he confessed to me that he felt warmly for Susan, and asked if I thought Sir Miles would consent. I knew too well how proud the poor old gentleman was, to give him any such hopes. So he left, very honourably. You remember, after he went, that Susan's spirits were low,—you remarked it."

"Yes, indeed, I remember. But when the first shock of Sir Miles's death was over, she got back her sweet colour, and looked cheerful enough."

"Because, perhaps, then she felt that she had a fortune to bestow on Mr.
Mainwaring, and thought all obstacle was over."

"Why, how clever you are! How did you get at her thoughts?"

"My own folly,—my own rash folly," almost groaned Mr. Fielden. "For not guessing that Mr. Mainwaring could have got engaged meanwhile to Lucretia, and suspecting how it was with Susan's poor little heart, I let out, in a jest—Heaven forgive me!—what William had said; and the dear child blushed, and kissed me, and—why, a day or two after, when it was fixed that we should come up to London, Lucretia informed me, with her freezing politeness, that she was to marry Mainwaring herself as soon as her first mourning was over."

"Poor, dear, dear Susan!"

"Susan behaved like an angel; and when I broached it to her, I thought she was calm; and I am sure she prayed with her whole heart that both might be happy."

"I'm sure she did. What is to be done? I understand it all now. Dear me, dear me! a sad piece of work indeed." And Mrs. Fielden abstractedly picked up the scissors.

"It was not till our coming to town, and Mr. Mainwaring's visits to Lucretia, that her strength gave way."


"A hard sight to bear,—I never could have borne it, my love. If I had seen you paying court to another, I should have—I don't know what I should have done! But what an artful wretch this young Mainwaring must be."

"Not very artful; for you see that he looks even sadder than Susan. He got entangled somehow, to be sure. Perhaps he had given up Susan in despair; and Miss Clavering, if haughty, is no doubt a very superior young lady; and, I dare say, it is only now in seeing them both together, and comparing the two, that he feels what a treasure he has lost. Well, what do you advise, Mary? Mainwaring, no doubt, is bound in honour to Miss Clavering; but she will be sure to discover, sooner or later, the state of his feelings, and then I tremble for both. I'm sure she will never be happy, while he will be wretched; and Susan—I dare not think upon Susan; she has a cough that goes to my heart."

"So she has; that cough—you don't know the money I spend on black- currant jelly! What's my advice? Why, I'd speak to Miss Clavering at once, if I dared. I'm sure love will never break her heart; and she's so proud, she'd throw him off without a sigh, if she knew how things stood."

"I believe you are right," said Mr. Fielden; "for truth is the best policy, after all. Still, it's scarce my business to meddle; and if it were not for Susan— Well, well, I must think of it, and pray Heaven to direct me."

This conference suffices to explain to the reader the stage to which the history of Lucretia had arrived. Willingly we pass over what it were scarcely possible to describe,—her first shock at the fall from the expectations of her life; fortune, rank, and what she valued more than either, power, crushed at a blow. From the dark and sullen despair into which she was first plunged, she was roused into hope, into something like joy, by Mainwaring's letters. Never had they been so warm and so tender; for the young man felt not only poignant remorse that he had been the cause of her downfall (though she broke it to him with more delicacy than might have been expected from the state of her feelings and the hardness of her character), but he felt also imperiously the obligations which her loss rendered more binding than ever. He persuaded, he urged, he forced himself into affection; and probably without a murmur of his heart, he would have gone with her to the altar, and, once wedded, custom and duty would have strengthened the chain imposed on himself, had it not been for Lucretia's fatal eagerness to see him, to come up to London, where she induced him to meet her,—for with her came Susan; and in Susan's averted face and trembling hand and mute avoidance of his eye, he read all which the poor dissembler fancied she concealed. But the die was cast, the union announced, the time fixed, and day by day he came to the house, to leave it in anguish and despair. A feeling they shared in common caused these two unhappy persons to shun each other. Mainwaring rarely came into the usual sitting-room of the family; and when be did so, chiefly in the evening, Susan usually took refuge in her own room. If they met, it was by accident, on the stairs, or at the sudden opening of a door; then not only no word, but scarcely even a look was exchanged: neither had the courage to face the other. Perhaps, of the two, this reserve weighed most on Susan; perhaps she most yearned to break the silence,—for she thought she divined the cause of Mainwaring's gloomy and mute constraint in the upbraidings of his conscience, which might doubtless recall, if no positive pledge to Susan, at least those words and tones which betray the one heart, and seek to allure the other; and the profound melancholy stamped on his whole person, apparent even to her hurried glance, touched her with a compassion free from all the bitterness of selfish reproach. She fancied she could die happy if she could remove that cloud from his brow, that shadow from his conscience. Die; for she thought not of life. She loved gently, quietly,—not with the vehement passion that belongs to stronger natures; but it was the love of which the young and the pure have died. The face of the Genius was calm and soft; and only by the lowering of the hand do you see that the torch burns out, and that the image too serene for earthly love is the genius of loving Death.

Absorbed in the egotism of her passion (increased, as is ever the case with women, even the worst, by the sacrifices it had cost her), and if that passion paused, by the energy of her ambition, which already began to scheme and reconstruct new scaffolds to repair the ruined walls of the past,—Lucretia as yet had not detected what was so apparent to the simple sense of Mr. Fielden. That Mainwaring was grave and thoughtful and abstracted, she ascribed only to his grief at the thought of her loss, and his anxieties for her altered future; and in her efforts to console him, her attempts to convince him that greatness in England did not consist only in lands and manors,—that in the higher walks of life which conduct to the Temple of Renown, the leaders of the procession are the aristocracy of knowledge and of intellect,—she so betrayed, not generous emulation and high-souled aspiring, but the dark, unscrupulous, tortuous ambition of cunning, stratagem, and intrigue, that instead of feeling grateful and encouraged, he shuddered and revolted. How, accompanied and led by a spirit which he felt to be stronger and more commanding than his own,—how preserve the whiteness of his soul, the uprightness of his honour? Already he felt himself debased. But in the still trial of domestic intercourse, with the daily, hourly dripping on the stone, in the many struggles between truth and falsehood, guile and candour, which men—and, above all, ambitious men—must wage, what darker angel would whisper him in his monitor? Still, he was bound,—bound with an iron band; he writhed, but dreamed not of escape.

The day after that of Fielden's conference with his wife, an unexpected visitor came to the house. Olivier Dalibard called. He had not seen Lucretia since she had left Laughton, nor had any correspondence passed between them. He came at dusk, just after Mainwaring's daily visit was over, and Lucretia was still in the parlour, which she had appropriated to herself. Her brow contracted as his name was announced, and the maid- servant lighted the candle on the table, stirred the fire, and gave a tug at the curtains. Her eye, glancing from his, round the mean room, with its dingy horsehair furniture, involuntarily implied the contrast between the past state and the present, which his sight could scarcely help to impress on her. But she welcomed him with her usual stately composure, and without reference to what had been. Dalibard was secretly anxious to discover if she suspected himself of any agency in the detection of the eventful letter; and assured by her manner that no such thought was yet harboured, he thought it best to imitate her own reserve. He assumed, however, a manner that, far more respectful than he ever before observed to his pupil, was nevertheless sufficiently kind and familiar to restore them gradually to their old footing; and that he succeeded was apparent, when, after a pause, Lucretia said abruptly: "How did Sir Miles St. John discover my correspondence with Mr. Mainwaring?"

"Is it possible that you are ignorant? Ah, how—how should you know it?" And Dalibard so simply explained the occurrence, in which, indeed, it was impossible to trace the hand that had moved springs which seemed so entirely set at work by an accident, that despite the extreme suspiciousness of her nature, Lucretia did not see a pretence for accusing him. Indeed, when he related the little subterfuge of Gabriel, his attempt to save her by taking the letter on himself, she felt thankful to the boy, and deemed Gabriel's conduct quite in keeping with his attachment to herself. And this accounted satisfactorily for the only circumstance that had ever troubled her with a doubt,—namely, the legacy left to Gabriel. She knew enough of Sir Miles to be aware that he would be grateful to any one who had saved the name of his niece, even while most embittered against her, from the shame attached to clandestine correspondence.

"It is strange, nevertheless," said she, thoughtfully, after a pause, "that the girl should have detected the letter, concealed as it was by the leaves that covered it."

"But," answered Dalibard, readily, "you see two or three persons had entered before, and their feet must have displaced the leaves."

"Possibly; the evil is now past recall."

"And Mr. Mainwaring? Do you still adhere to one who has cost you so much, poor child?"

"In three months more I shall be his wife."

Dalibard sighed deeply, but offered no remonstrance.

"Well," he said, taking her hand with mingled reverence and affection, — "well, I oppose your inclinations no more, for now there is nothing to risk; you are mistress of your own fortune; and since Mainwaring has talents, that fortune will suffice for a career. Are you at length convinced that I have conquered my folly; that I was disinterested when I incurred your displeasure? If so, can you restore to me your friendship? You will have some struggle with the world, and, with my long experience of men and life, even I, the poor exile, may assist you."

And so thought Lucretia; for with some dread of Dalibard's craft, she yet credited his attachment to herself, and she felt profound admiration for an intelligence more consummate and accomplished than any ever yet submitted to her comprehension. From that time, Dalibard became an habitual visitor at the house; he never interfered with Lucretia's interviews with Mainwaring; he took the union for granted, and conversed with her cheerfully on the prospects before her; he ingratiated himself with the Fieldens, played with the children, made himself at home, and in the evenings when Mainwaring, as often as he could find the excuse, absented himself from the family circle, he contrived to draw Lucretia into more social intercourse with her homely companions than she had before condescended to admit. Good Mr. Fielden rejoiced; here was the very person, — the old friend of Sir Miles, the preceptor of Lucretia herself, evidently most attached to her, having influence over her, — the very person to whom to confide his embarrassment. One day, therefore, when Dalibard had touched his heart by noticing the paleness of Susan, he took him aside and told him all. "And now," concluded the pastor, hoping he had found one to relieve him of his dreaded and ungracious task, "don't you think that I — or rather you — as so old a friend, should speak frankly to Miss Clavering herself?"

"No, indeed," said the Provencal, quickly; "if we spoke to her, she would disbelieve us. She would no doubt appeal to Mainwaring, and Mainwaring would have no choice but to contradict us. Once put on his guard, he would control his very sadness. Lucretia, offended, might leave your house, and certainly she would regard her sister as having influenced your confession, — a position unworthy Miss Mivers. But do not fear: if the evil be so, it carries with it its inevitable remedy. Let Lucretia discover it herself; but, pardon me, she must have seen, at your first reception of Mainwaring, that he had before been acquainted with you?"

"She was not in the room when we first received Mainwaring; and I have always been distant to him, as you may suppose, for I felt disappointed and displeased. Of course, however, she is aware that we knew him before she did. What of that?"

"Why, do you think, then, he told her at Laughton of this acquaintance, — that he spoke of Susan? I suspect not."

"I cannot say, I am sure," said Mr. Fielden.

"Ask her that question accidentally; and for the rest, be discreet, my dear sir. I thank you for your confidence. I will watch well over my poor young pupil. She must not, indeed, be sacrificed to a man whose affections are engaged elsewhere."

Dalibard trod on air as he left the house; his very countenance had changed; he seemed ten years younger. It was evening; and suddenly, as he came into Oxford Street, he encountered a knot of young men — noisy and laughing loud — obstructing the pavement, breaking jests on the more sober passengers, and attracting the especial and admiring attention of sundry ladies in plumed hats and scarlet pelisses; for the streets then enjoyed a gay liberty which has vanished from London with the lanterns of the watchmen. Noisiest and most conspicuous of these descendants of the Mohawks, the sleek and orderly scholar beheld the childish figure of his son. Nor did Gabriel shrink from his father's eye, stern and scornful as it was, but rather braved the glance with an impudent leer.

Right, however, in the midst of the group, strode the Provencal, and laying his hand very gently on the boy's shoulder, he said: "My son, come with me."

Gabriel looked irresolute, and glanced at his companions. Delighted at the prospect of a scene, they now gathered round, with countenances and gestures that seemed little disposed to acknowledge the parental authority.

"Gentlemen," said Dalibard, turning a shade more pale, for though morally most resolute, physically he was not brave,— "gentlemen, I must beg you to excuse me; this child is my son!"

"But Art is his mother," replied a tall, raw-boned young man, with long tawny hair streaming down from a hat very much battered. "At the juvenile age, the child is consigned to the mother! Have I said it?" and he turned round theatrically to his comrades.

"Bravo!" cried the rest, clapping their hands.

"Down with all tyrants and fathers! hip, hip, Hurrah!" and the hideous diapason nearly split the drum of the ears into which it resounded.

"Gabriel," whispered the father, "you had better follow me, had you not?
Reflect!" So saying, he bowed low to the unpropitious assembly, and as
if yielding the victory, stepped aside and crossed over towards Bond
Street.


Before the din of derision and triumph died away, Dalibard looked back, and saw Gabriel behind him.

"Approach, sir," he said; and as the boy stood still, he added, "I promise peace if you will accept it."

"Peace, then," answered Gabriel, and he joined his father's side.

"So," said Dalibard, "when I consented to your studying Art, as you call it, under your mother's most respectable brother, I ought to have contemplated what would be the natural and becoming companions of the rising Raphael I have given to the world."

"I own, sir," replied Gabriel, demurely, "that they are riotous fellows; but some of them are clever, and —"

"And excessively drunk," interrupted Dalibard, examining the gait of his son. "Do you learn that accomplishment also, by way of steadying your hand for the easel?"

"No, sir; I like wine well enough, but I would not be drunk for the world. I see people when they are drunk are mere fools, — let out their secrets, and show themselves up."

"Well said," replied the father, almost admiringly. "But a truce with this bantering, Gabriel. Can you imagine that I will permit you any longer to remain with that vagabond Varney and yon crew of vauriens? You will come home with me; and if you must be a painter, I will look out for a more trustworthy master."

"I shall stay where I am," answered Gabriel, firmly, and compressing his lips with a force that left them bloodless.

"What, boy? Do I hear right? Dare you disobey me? Dare you defy?"

"Not in your house, so I will not enter it again." Dalibard laughed mockingly.

"Peste! but this is modest! You are not of age yet, Mr. Varney; you are not free from a father's tyrannical control."

"The law does not own you as my father, I am told, sir. You have said my name rightly, — it is Varney, not Dalibard. We have no rights over each other; so at least says Tom Passmore, and his father's a lawyer!"

Dalibard's hand griped his son's arm fiercely. Despite his pain, which was acute, the child uttered no cry; but he growled beneath his teeth, "Beware! beware! or my mother's son may avenge her death!"

Dalibard removed his hand, and staggered as if struck. Gliding from his side, Gabriel seized the occasion to escape; he paused, however, midway in the dull, lamp-lit kennel when he saw himself out of reach, and then approaching cautiously, said: "I know. I am a boy, but you have made me man enough to take care of myself. Mr. Varney, my uncle, will maintain me; when of age, old Sir Miles has provided for me. Leave me in peace, treat me as free, and I will visit you, help you when you want me, obey you still, — yes, follow your instructions; for I know you are," he paused, "you are wise. But if you seek again to make me your slave, you will only find your foe. Good-night; and remember that a bastard has no father!"

With these words he moved on, and hurrying down the street, turned the corner and vanished.

Dalibard remained motionless for some minutes; at length he muttered: "Ay, let him go, he is dangerous! What son ever revolted even from the worst father, and throve in life? Food for the gibbet! What matters?"

When next Dalibard visited Lucretia, his manner was changed; the cheerfulness he had before assumed gave place to a kind of melancholy compassion; he no longer entered into her plans for the future, but would look at her mournfully, start up, and walk away. She would have attributed the change to some return of his ancient passion, but she heard him once murmur with unspeakable pity, "Poor child, poor child!" A vague apprehension seized her, — first, indeed, caught from some remarks dropped by Mr. Fielden, which were less discreet than Dalibard had recommended. A day or two afterwards, she asked Mainwaring, carelessly, why he had never spoken to her at Laughton of his acquaintance with Fielden.

"You asked me that before," he said, somewhat sullenly.

"Did I? I forget! But how was it? Tell me again."

"I scarcely know," he replied confusedly; "we were always talking of each other or poor Sir Miles, — our own hopes and fears."

This was true, and a lover's natural excuse. In the present of love all the past is forgotten.

"Still," said Lucretia, with her sidelong glance, — "still, as you must have seen much of my own sister — "

Mainwaring, while she spoke, was at work on a button on his gaiter (gaiters were then worn tight at the ankle); the effort brought the blood to his forehead.

"But," he said, still stooping at his occupation, "you were so little intimate with your sister; I feared to offend. Family differences are so difficult to approach."

Lucretia was satisfied at the moment; for so vast was her stake in Mainwaring's heart, so did her whole heart and soul grapple to the rock left serene amidst the deluge, that she habitually and resolutely thrust from her mind all the doubts that at times invaded it.

"I know," she would often say to herself, — "I know he does not love as I do; but man never can, never ought to love as woman! Were I a man, I should scorn myself if I could be so absorbed in one emotion as I am proud to be now, — I, poor woman! I know," again she would think, — "I know how suspicious and distrustful I am; I must not distrust him, — I shall only irritate, I may lose him: I dare not distrust, — it would be too dreadful."

Thus, as a system vigorously embraced by a determined mind, she had schooled and forced herself into reliance on her lover. His words now, we say, satisfied her at the moment; but afterwards, in absence, they were recalled, in spite of herself, — in the midst of fears, shapeless and undefined. Involuntarily she began to examine the countenance, the movements, of her sister, — to court Susan's society more than she had done; for her previous indifference had now deepened into bitterness. Susan, the neglected and despised, had become her equal, — nay, more than her equal: Susan's children would have precedence to her own in the heritage of Laughton! Hitherto she had never deigned to talk to her in the sweet familiarity of sisters so placed; never deigned to confide to her those feelings for her future husband which burned lone and ardent in the close vault of her guarded heart. Now, however, she began to name him, wind her arm into Susan's, talk of love and home, and the days to come; and as she spoke, she read the workings of her sister's face. That part of the secret grew clear almost at the first glance. Susan loved, — loved William Mainwaring; but was it not a love hopeless and unreturned? Might not this be the cause that had made Mainwaring so reserved? He might have seen, or conjectured, a conquest he had not sought; and hence, with manly delicacy, he had avoided naming Susan to Lucretia; and now, perhaps, sought the excuses which at times had chafed and wounded her for not joining the household circle. If one of those who glance over these pages chances to be a person more than usually able and acute, — a person who has loved and been deceived, — he or she, no matter which, will perhaps recall those first moments when the doubt, long put off, insisted to be heard. A weak and foolish heart gives way to the doubt at once; not so the subtler and more powerful, — it rather, on the contrary, recalls all the little circumstances that justify trust and make head against suspicion; it will not render the citadel at the mere sound of the trumpet; it arms all its forces, and bars its gates on the foe. Hence it is that the persons most easy to dupe in matters of affection are usually those most astute in the larger affairs of life. Moliere, reading every riddle in the vast complexities of human character, and clinging, in self-imposed credulity, to his profligate wife, is a type of a striking truth. Still, a foreboding, a warning instinct withheld Lucretia from plumbing farther into the deeps of her own fears. So horrible was the thought that she had been deceived, that rather than face it, she would have preferred to deceive herself. This poor, bad heart shrank from inquiry, it trembled at the idea of condemnation. She hailed, with a sentiment of release that partook of rapture, Susan's abrupt announcement one morning that she had accepted an invitation from some relations of her father to spend some time with them at their villa near Hampstead; she was to go the end of the week. Lucretia hailed it, though she saw the cause, — Susan shrank from the name of Mainwaring on Lucretia's lips; shrank from the familiar intercourse so ruthlessly forced on her! With a bright eye, that day, Lucretia met her lover; yet she would not tell him of Susan's intended departure, she had not the courage.

Dalibard was foiled. This contradiction in Lucretia's temper, so suspicious, so determined, puzzled even his penetration. He saw that bolder tactics were required. He waylaid Mainwaring on the young man's way to his lodgings, and after talking to him on indifferent matters, asked him carelessly whether he did not think Susan far gone in a decline. Affecting not to notice the convulsive start with which the question was received, he went on, —

"There is evidently something on her mind; I observe that her eyes are often red, as with weeping, poor girl. Perhaps some silly love-affair. However, we shall not see her again before your marriage; she is going away in a day or two. The change of air may possibly yet restore her, — I own, though, I fear the worst. At this time of the year, and in your climate, such complaints as I take hers to be are rapid. Good-day. We may meet this evening."

Terror-stricken at these barbarous words, Mainwaring no sooner reached his lodging than he wrote and despatched a note to Fielden, entreating him to call.

The vicar obeyed the summons, and found Mainwaring in a state of mind bordering on distraction. Nor when Susan was named did Fielden's words take the shape of comfort; for he himself was seriously alarmed for her health. The sound of her low cough rang in his ears, and he rather heightened than removed the picture which haunted Mainwaring, — Susan stricken, dying, broken-hearted!

Tortured both in heart and conscience, Mainwaring felt as if he had but one wish left in the world, — to see Susan once more. What to say, he scarce knew; but for her to depart, — depart perhaps to her grave, believing him coldly indifferent, — for her not to know at least his struggles, and pronounce his pardon, was a thought beyond endurance. After such an interview both would have new fortitude, — each would unite in encouraging the other in the only step left to honour. And this desire he urged upon Fielden with all the eloquence of passionate grief as he entreated him to permit and procure one last conference with Susan. But this, the plain sense and straightforward conscience of the good man long refused. If Mainwaring had been left in the position to explain his heart to Lucretia, it would not have been for Fielden to object; but to have a clandestine interview with one sister while betrothed to the other, bore in itself a character too equivocal to meet with the simple vicar's approval.

"What can you apprehend?" exclaimed the young man, almost fiercely; for, harassed and tortured, his mild nature was driven to bay. "Can you suppose that I shall encourage my own misery by the

guilty pleadings of unavailing love? All that I ask is the luxury —
yes, the luxury, long unknown to me, of candour — to place fairly
and manfully before Susan the position in which fate has involved
me. Can you suppose that we shall not both take comfort and
strength from each other? Our duty is plain and obvious; but it
grows less painful, encouraged by the lips of a companion in suffering. I tell you fairly that see Susan I will and must. I will watch
round her home, wherever it be, hour after hour; come what may, I
will find my occasion. Is it not better that the interview should be
under your roof, within the same walls which shelter her sister?
There, the place itself imposes restraint on despair. Oh, sir, this is no
time for formal scruples; be merciful, I beseech you, not to me, but
to Susan. I judge of her by myself. I know that I shall go to the altar
more resigned to the future if for once I can give vent to what
weighs upon my heart. She will then see, as I do, that the path before me is inevitable; she will compose herself to face the fate that
compels us. We shall swear tacitly to each other, not to love, but to
conquer love. Believe me, sir, I am not selfish in this prayer; an instinct, the intuition which human grief has into the secrets of human
grief, assures me that that which I ask is the best consolation you
can afford to Susan. You own she is ill, — suffering. Are not your
fears for her very life — O Heaven? for her very life — gravely awa-
kened? And yet you see we have been silent to each other! Can speech be more fatal in its results than silence? Oh, for her sake, hear
me!"

The good man's tears fell fast. His scruples were shaken; there
was truth in what Mainwaring urged. He did not yield, but he promised to reflect, and inform Mainwaring, by a line, in the evening.
Finding this was all he could effect, the young man at last suffered
him to leave the house, and Fielden hastened to take counsel of
Dalibard; that wily persuader soon reasoned away Mr. Fielden's last
faint objection. It now only remained to procure Susan's assent to
the interview, and to arrange that it should be undisturbed. Mr.
Fielden should take out the children the next morning. Dalibard
volunteered to contrive the absence of Lucretia at the hour ap-
pointed. Mrs. Fielden alone should remain within, and might, if it
were judged proper, be present at the interview, which was fixed
for the forenoon in the usual drawing-room. Nothing but Susan's

consent was now necessary, and Mr. Fielden ascended to her room. He knocked twice,—no sweet voice bade him enter; he opened the door gently,—Susan was in prayer. At the opposite corner of the room, by the side of her bed, she knelt, her face buried in her hands, and he heard, low and indistinct, the murmur broken by the sob. But gradually, as he stood unperceived, sob and murmur ceased,—prayer had its customary and blessed effect with the pure and earnest. And when Susan rose, though the tears yet rolled down her cheeks, the face was serene as an angel's.

The pastor approached and took her hand; a blush then broke o-ver her countenance,—she trembled, and her eyes fell on the ground. "My child," he said solemnly, "God will hear you!" And after those words there was a long silence. He then drew her passively towards a seat, and sat down by her, embarrassed how to begin. At length he said, looking somewhat aside, "Mr. Mainwaring has made me a request,—a prayer which relates to you, and which I refer to you. He asks you to grant him an interview before you leave us,—to-morrow, if you will. I refused at first,—I am in doubt still; for, my dear, I have always found that when the feelings move us, our duty becomes less clear to the human heart,—corrupt, we know, but still it is often a safer guide than our reason. I never knew reason unerring, except in mathematics; we have no Euclid," and the good man smiled mournfully, "in the problems of real life. I will not urge you one way or the other; I put the case before you: Would it, as the young man says, give you comfort and strength to see him once again while, while—in short, before your sister is—I mean before—that is, would it soothe you now, to have an unreserved communication with him? He implores it. What shall I answer?"

"This trial, too!" muttered Susan, almost inaudibly,—"this trial which I once yearned for; "and the hand clasped in Fielden's was as cold as ice. Then, turning her eyes to her guardian somewhat wildly, she cried: "But to what end, what object? Why should he wish to see me?"

"To take greater courage to do his duty; to feel less unhappy at— at—"

"I will see him," interrupted Susan, firmly,—"he is right; it will strengthen both. I will see him!"

"But human nature is weak, my child; if my heart be so now, what will be yours?"

"Fear me not," answered Susan, with a sad, wandering smile; and she repeated vacantly: "I will see him!"

The good man looked at her, threw his arms round her wasted form, and lifting up his eyes, his lips stirred with such half-syllabled words as fathers breathe on high.